WITCH IN DANGER

A BLAIR WILKES MYSTERY

ELLE ADAMS

———

I looked down at the slip of paper, clutching my phone in my free hand. Suddenly, the idea of calling my foster parents seemed as daunting as mounting a broomstick for the first time. Because on the slip of paper was a message from my birth family.

The note simply said,

To Blair,

I would very much like to meet you.

Please come to the waterfall at the solstice.

Sincerely,

Your family.

I'd read every word so many times, it was a wonder they hadn't faded from the page. *Your family...* and no signature. Since my foster parents didn't even know I was now living in the magical town of Fairy Falls, I had no name to trace the note back to, and by now, I'd grown desperate enough to call Mr and Mrs Wilkes in the hope that they remembered more than they'd told me of my birth family.

I swallowed my fear and dialled my foster dad's number. Mr and Mrs Wilkes might be my real parents in all but blood, but they were a hundred percent normal and had never met either of my birth parents. They were now enjoying their retirement in Australia, blissfully unaware that I'd spent the last couple of months accidentally investigating magical murders, making badly timed Harry Potter references, and generally running into trouble. My mother had been a witch who'd originally lived here in my new home of Fairy Falls, but she'd left over twenty-five years ago, before she was pregnant with me. My father, on the other hand, nobody knew at all. Not even Vincent the vampire, the town's oldest resident. But someone had left that note for me, and in the weeks since, doubt had festered until I was scared to call my foster parents at all—since I also happened to have the magical ability to sense whether or not someone was lying. And I didn't know how to handle it if it turned out they knew.

Before I lost my nerve, I hit the call button.

"Blair?" Mr Wilkes answered, after a few moments.

"Hi," I said. "How's it going?"

He launched into tales of his adventures—which involved learning to surf—while I smiled and said "mm" every so often. When I got a moment to speak, the words stuck in my throat, but I pushed ahead. "This is kind of random, but I wondered... did you ever hear from my birth parents? At all?"

"No," he said, sounding puzzled. "What brought this on?"

"Just... curiosity." *Great one, Blair.* I was trying—unsuccessfully—to break my habit of telling little white lies, but there were rules against telling normals about the paranormal world, even family. I had absolutely no idea what I was going to do when they returned from their travels and found I'd moved to a town that didn't exist on any normal map. "Er, since they never got in touch."

There was an awkward silence. We hadn't often discussed the subject since I was a kid, because once I'd passed the stage of making up elaborate stories as to why they might not have contacted me—involving superhero identities and secret societies, among other things—I'd concluded that I had all the family I wanted. But since I'd moved here, old wounds I'd never acknowledged had been opened.

"Blair," Mr Wilkes finally said. "If you really want to know, I can give you the details of your former foster family. I don't know how well you remember them."

'Not well' was the honest answer. I'd had several foster families before Mr and Mrs Wilkes, and they had probably been plain humans, too. I doubted the human authorities kept a record of where exactly I'd come from if my parents had hopped over from the magical world and worked their magic to leave no trace. Unless... unless *they'd* been hiding amongst normals, keeping their magic quiet, before I was born. It wasn't like some paranormals didn't opt to spend their lives in normal towns or cities.

"Did they really live in London?" I blurted. "My birth parents, I mean?" London, with its traffic and crowds, did not seem like a good place for paranormals whose natural magical shields often made public transport shut down. But a big city like that *would* be a decent place to hide without most people having a clue someone might be paranormal. I'd lived there for a few weeks when I'd snagged a fancy office job a couple of years ago, but I didn't have the funds to stay after my contract finished. And the tube breaking down every day hadn't helped much. At least I now knew it was down to my magical nature and not just bad luck.

"That's all we were told. Your last foster family might know."

Since a few different families had taken me in before the age of three, it was possible that none of them would have actually met my parents. When you added in the fact that paranormals were capable of befuddling the senses and causing people to forget ever meeting them… the odds were slim, I had to admit.

"I, er, got another job offer," I said, to fill the silence. "So I moved."

"You did? What's the job?"

"Recruitment," I said—technically true, if you omitted the 'dealing with cranky wizard businessmen and eccentric witches' part. "I'm not living at my last address anymore, but I'll come and see you when you get back."

"We'll come back for Grandma's seventieth birthday," he said.

Oh. My adoptive grandparents must have sent the invitation to my old house—which I'd left after I moved here.

"Okay. I'll let you know when I'm around," I said. "But, er, it's probably best not to post anything to me. I don't have a fixed address."

Not an address that ordinary humans could find, anyway. There was a paranormal delivery company within Fairy Falls and even a phone and internet network, but they didn't work outside of the town. I'd barely spoken to anyone from my old life, not even my former best friend, Rebecca. She only got in touch when she wanted me to babysit for her the last couple of years and we'd grown apart, and I wasn't perpetually short on cash anymore. I had a steady job I loved. I had great co-workers and a fantastic new best friend, and a patient mentor who forgave me every time I messed up a spell or accidentally broke something.

I had a family. And I had a whole new life, and yet— was it such a bad thing that I wanted to know the truth about my parents?

"See you soon, Blair. Love you."

"Love you," I whispered back.

I ended the call, blinked a few times to clear the tears from my eyes, then put my phone away and looked at the note. I'd read it so many times that the words were burned into my brain. No signature. Anyone might have written it, in theory, but the note had been glamoured, hidden with fairy magic. I didn't have many enemies— except possibly Blythe, my vindictive former co-worker— and none were fairies. Nobody would have reason to prank me into thinking I'd get to meet my family, right?

"Anything?" asked Alissa, my flatmate, as I walked out of my room and re-entered the living room of our shared flat.

I shook my head. "Nope. I really don't think they know. But if they come home and want to visit me... that might cause problems."

She petted Roald, her cat. "Ah. Yeah, you might want to ask Madame Grey. Pretty sure she has a script for telling normals about us without *really* telling them anything, if you know what I mean."

"This would... confuse them." To be honest, I still

spent half my time in a permanent state of confusion even now I'd had weeks to grow used to this new life. "I'll think about it."

The note had told me to meet at the solstice… and now the day was finally here. In the last few weeks, I'd thrown myself into magic lessons and work, and when Veronica had given me last weekend off, Alissa and I had ended up helping to lay a pirate's ghost to rest, and found out that my cat was actually buddies with the town's oldest vampire resident. Life was busy, in the best way, and I almost didn't want to disrupt it by throwing my forgotten history into the mix.

"Are you definitely going to go to the falls? At night?" she asked.

"Yeah. Might be a prank, but at least I'll know."

I'd been dreaming of the meeting for weeks. When I'd stuck my own head under the Fairy Falls, the glamour masking my real appearance had temporarily come off, revealing wings, and… since I hadn't looked in a mirror and Alissa had just said I was glittering, my imagination filled in the blanks. The fairies had been responsible for creating the Fairy Falls that gave the town its name, but had disappeared decades ago. That alone gave the meeting place extra significance—but the note hadn't explained why the writer had picked the solstice.

"Aren't you seeing Nathan tonight first?"

I nodded, biting my lip. I still hadn't actually told him I was half fairy. And now I was running out of time to make my decision about how to broach the subject.

"How many dates have you had now?" Alissa enquired.

"Two, but neither of them was an actual date, and both

got interrupted. No, I'm not counting the coffee shop incident."

"I'll bet *he* is."

"Considering the cat interrupted our first date and a murder interrupted the second one, I'd be genuinely surprised if the ceiling doesn't fall on us tonight."

"The lucky latte's backlash has probably worn off by now."

"I should hope so." I'd drank a luck potion in order to solve a murder and the backlash had lasted for days. After endless problem clients, magical accidents, and disastrous attempts to cast spells, I was looking forward to a stress-free night out with Nathan, retired paranormal hunter, town security guard, and the one person I did *not* want to know about my midnight meeting.

I know, I know. Keeping secrets from the guy you're sort-of-dating is bound to end badly. That he'd hunted the same paranormals who might be my relations didn't help, either. As a paranormal hunter, it'd been his job to apprehend any and all criminals he was assigned to, from rogue werewolves to vamps who took a bite out of a human— and fairies who bewitched normals. I hadn't got up the courage to ask too many questions about his former job. It wasn't exactly a sore subject, there just never seemed to be a good time, since we were surrounded by paranormals constantly who wouldn't appreciate being reminded. Nathan seemed to get on with the others just fine—with the glaring exception of the werewolf pack—so I didn't want to make things awkward for him. All I really knew about his life now was that he had a sister and three cats. It was no wonder *have you ever met any fairies* had never come up as a question.

Since I'd graduated from university, dating opportunities had all but vanished as everyone settled down and I carried on drifting, looking for... something. I might have only been here a couple of months, but it felt like longer, and I couldn't imagine being elsewhere. The ease with which I'd fallen into this life had bothered me a little at first, but now it comforted me.

My phone buzzed with a message.

"Is that him?" Alissa asked.

"Yes." I looked at the phone, my heart sinking in disappointment. "He's cancelled. I guess something security-related came up."

I wasn't really surprised. Everyone wanted to hire the town's only retired paranormal hunter to guard their valuables, and I couldn't help feeling slightly relieved that there was less chance of him finding out about my midnight tryst. And then wondering what that said about our potential relationship. *I want to tell him. Just not now. Not before I find out who wanted to meet me.* If someone was out to play a practical joke, I didn't want him to see the fallout. I wanted to keep my weird history and my witchy future firmly apart.

Alissa checked her watch. "I should get to my shift. Night shifts on a Friday should be illegal."

"Someone has to stop the alcoholic elf escaping to the liquor store or the blood-crazed vampires from feasting on unsuspecting humans." I gave her a wry smile. Alissa worked at the local hospital as a healer, and her working hours were becoming more and more irregular as summer went on and the number of people taking stupid risks soared.

She groaned. "Don't even. That elf is the bane of my

existence. Anyway, I need to go. I can meet you by the lake at eleven thirty? I wouldn't stand too close to the water at night."

"I'll meet you there." I'd have to find some other way to distract myself from my upcoming meeting until midnight.

"Miaow," said Sky the cat, padding into the room. He was a little black cat with a single white paw, and large eyes—one grey, one blue.

"You think I'm making the right choice?" I asked him.

"Miaow."

"Me neither." I didn't really understand my familiar, since his vocabulary consisted only of one word. Besides, Alissa had said it wasn't generally a good idea to ask for life advice from a cat.

Sighing, I relaxed back into the sofa, wishing I had a television or some other entertainment. Alissa's grandmother had given her a traditional technology-free upbringing despite the fact that paranormals had found ways to replicate normal inventions using their magic. I appreciated the paranormal phone network, but considering everyone in town lived so close to one another, I didn't get as much use out of it as I might.

I stroked Sky's head, and he purred, pleased to be getting his fair share of attention. He and Roald had stopped swatting at each other most of the time and now treated one another with indifference. Fiercely independent and demanding, Sky was like another flatmate all by himself.

I was dozing off when Sky suddenly jolted upright. His fur stood on end. "Miaow."

"What is it?"

Sky bounded off the sofa and ran towards the door.

"Who, an intruder?" I didn't think so. Several other families lived inside the house, since it was big enough to contain more than one flat per floor. "Or more mice?"

Please no more mice.

He hit out at the door with his paw. "MIAOW."

"Oh, all right, I'm coming."

I grabbed my handbag, shoved my feet into my boots, and hurried after him. Sky knocked open the door, ran into the hallway, and barely gave me the chance to lock the flat door before shoving his way through the cat flap and out into the night.

I followed close behind. "I don't have to leave until midnight."

Normally walking around at night alone would have made me hesitate, but I wore a pair of levitating boots, carried a wand, and the town was the safest place I'd ever lived in. This whole area belonged to Madame Grey and her coven, and she didn't allow any trouble to walk up to her doorstep.

Sky kept running, turning the street corner. He was heading towards the bustling area of town. "You should have just told me I needed a night out."

The little black cat kept running past the pubs and night clubs, towards—

"The hospital?"

"Miaow."

I stopped. "Does Alissa need my help? How in the world did you know?"

"Miaow," he said, urgently pointing with his white paw.

I continued towards the hospital on the high street. I'd

spent some time there recently when I'd been questioning old Ava, a witch who lived in the ward for those with permanent magical injuries. If Alissa needed my help, she might have called or texted, but while Sky was unreliable, he *had* known a bunch of cursed mice were actually human. What if he was right about Alissa needing my help, too?

Through the dim glass, a number of people had gathered just inside the reception area, chief of whom was the huge, intimidating Steve the gargoyle—leader of the local police force.

Oh no. Recently, he'd caught me at a crime scene and locked me up for it. I'd been avoiding him for weeks.

Then I spotted the person in handcuffs next to him.

Alissa.

2

I pushed open the doors to the hospital and entered without stopping to think. Nobody noticed me at first, since their attention was on the gargoyle and his prisoner.

"I didn't do it," said Alissa, her face pale and her expression distraught. "You must know I didn't."

"A vampire was killed," said Steve, his voice harsh. "You were the last person in the room. And it looks like your accomplice just showed up."

Now everyone looked at me. Worse, Steve wasn't the only gargoyle present. Huge and muscular, with greying hair, he reminded me of stone cliffs and had an expression to match.

"You're being ridiculous," said one of Alissa's co-workers. "Everyone uses that room. And Blair... what is Blair doing here?"

"My familiar dragged me here," I said. "After Alissa. Just what is going on?"

"They found a body," Alissa said.

"Er," I said. "Not to sound insensitive, but isn't the hospital one of the few places where it's *not* unusual to find a dead body?"

"The dead man was a vampire," responded one of the gargoyles.

"Er… they're already dead, right?" This was not going well. But if I didn't figure out what had yanked the gargoyle's chain, Alissa might be locked in a cell overnight. That wasn't an experience I'd wish on anyone.

"The vampire was poisoned," said the gargoyle. "Specifically, by poison in the blood bank. The last person to go into that room was your friend."

My heart sank. Surely nobody would think Alissa was a murderer. No way.

"It might have been an accident," said the nurse who'd spoken, a young Asian woman around my age. "Vampires are immune to a lot of things that are poisonous to humans. Someone might have put it into the blood supply or dropped it…"

"You don't *accidentally* put poison in the blood supply," said Steve. "This was murder." To say the guy was a little trigger-happy when it came to arresting people first and asking questions later was an understatement. *Not Alissa. She would never.*

"Who exactly was it who died?" I asked.

"One of our oldest vampire residents, Lord Goddard."

Not Vincent, I thought, with some relief. Not that I necessarily *liked* the slightly creepy leading vampire—who was capable of mind-reading, among other things—but he was the only vampire I was on friendly speaking terms with. And he was also friends with my cat.

Wait. Maybe that's how Sky had known Alissa was in

trouble. I didn't think Vincent could read minds over a distance, let alone telepathically communicate with my not-quite-familiar, but it made more sense than the alternatives. Sky was definitely more magical than he let on, at any rate.

"This vampire was here to get blood?" I asked.

"Of course," said the nurse. "The vamps come and go all the time, so nobody pays too much attention when one of them uses the blood bank. He was found dead in the corridor. The effects came on fast."

"Which was no doubt the plan," snapped Steve the Gargoyle. "Nobody would question finding a dead body in a hospital. Vampire or not."

"Actually, they would," said the nurse. "Vampires don't get sick and rarely die. Unless they're deprived of blood, but this is the primary source in town."

That fit with what I knew. I'd only run into Vincent here before, but most vampires used the blood bank.

"Whoever it is knew how to kill an immortal," said Steve. "That means they must be arrested and apprehended immediately to protect the other residents of the town."

Ah. That's why he was freaked out. Killing a vampire was something even a stone-fisted gargoyle wasn't capable of. In fact, I'd thought the vampires had no weaknesses at all.

"The vampires have a lot of enemies," said Alissa. "Certainly, the older ones do."

"If you mean the werewolves, didn't you date one once?" asked the gargoyle closest to the doors, a brutish woman with thick dark hair.

Alissa flushed. "What does my love life have to do with anything?"

Steve's eyes gleamed and he loomed over Alissa. "Did a werewolf put you up to this?"

"You're being absurd," she said. "I didn't murder him. I'd have no reason to. And I'm not currently in contact with the werewolf pack."

Indignation surged within me on her behalf, and it was tempting to point my malfunctioning wand in the general direction of the gargoyle and 'accidentally' make him grow a tail for poking his nose into Alissa's private life. It still bewildered me a little that Alissa had dated the beta of the local pack, considering his hobby was playing the guitar for the possible worst band in the entire paranormal world. But that was none of the gargoyles' business. Vampires were known for being paranoid, particularly where the werewolves were concerned, but I wanted Alissa away from the case before she ended up locked in jail.

"Alissa would have traces of the poison on her if she did it," I pointed out. "And blood. Right?"

"Or," said the nurse, "is it possible one of the donors was poisoned beforehand and we only found out today?"

"Someone would have noticed," another nurse put in. "That blood has been there for days, at least, but it can be tested by a strong divining spell."

"That's up to the witches." Steve didn't move, remaining behind Alissa. "In the meantime, we need to take in the suspect as a precaution."

"She hasn't done anything to implicate herself as a suspect," I said. "There are dozens of other people who use that room, right? Did she even know the guy?"

Alissa shot me a grateful look. "No, I can't say I personally knew him."

"There you have it. No motive." I was trying to speak to Steve on his level, but his level was stubborn-as-a-rock and when he was on a mission, nothing would deter him.

At that moment, Vincent glided into the room, causing all attention to abruptly turn in his direction. "It seems a friend of mine has been murdered."

There was a moment's pause while everyone took in the vampire's sudden appearance. His skin was icy pale, with the appearance of one of those almost-realistic-looking wax models. His tar-black hair made him look even paler and he wore a dark suit, like he'd walked out of a handbook describing what vampires were supposed to look like. He alternated between gloomy, cryptic, and creepily seductive, depending on the day of the week. I'd never thought I'd be glad to see him.

I glanced down to my feet in search of Sky, but he wasn't there. Must have run back home, if he had any sense. I never did understand that cat.

Vincent's gaze travelled across the gathered staff, along with a few patients who'd clearly sneaked in to see what was going on, and the grim-faced gargoyles. His scan of the room ended on Steve, who hovered behind Alissa as though he planned to send her right to the gallows. I couldn't help myself from trying to catch his eye, but as a mind-reader, he'd likely have picked up on the situation—and Alissa's innocence—the moment he entered the room.

"Vincent." Steve gave him a nod that almost bordered on respectful. I blinked in surprise. I guessed even the chief of police showed deference to the town's oldest resident. "I suppose you heard?"

"Through several means."

A shiver went through the crowd as though everyone was trying hard not to imagine what those means might be.

"None of the people in this room committed the murder," Vincent announced.

Steve looked as though Christmas had been cancelled. "In that case," he said, addressing the nearest nurse, "contact all staff who aren't currently here but who might have been in the room today. In the meantime, I will question everyone who was near the donor room before his death."

Alissa made an indignant noise. "You don't want to distress the patients—"

"The killer might still be in the building!" said the female gargoyle beside the door. "In one of the other wards."

Alissa moved to follow the gargoyles leaving the room, but Steve blocked the way.

At the same moment, the vampire took a casual step towards him. "Have you any evidence against that woman?" he asked.

"No," Steve growled. Despite his furious expression, the vampire clearly rattled him. I stored that information away to tease him with later, and to my intense relief, Steve removed the handcuffs from Alissa and followed the other gargoyles. Several had caused a bottleneck in the corridor, their path blocked by nurses yelling, "This is a hospital! Keep the noise down!"

Freed from her handcuffs, Alissa made her way over to me. "Blair. What are you doing here?"

"Sky," I said. "He dragged me here. Must have known. He and the vampire are friends—" I broke off as said vampire turned to face us.

Alissa took a step backwards, out of the vampire's range. Vincent moved faster than ordinary people did and made little effort to hide it. While he seemed to have formed a weird friendship with my cat, that didn't mean he liked either of us personally, but he had just spared Alissa a night in a jail cell.

"Er, thank you," Alissa said tentatively.

"It took no great effort," he said dismissively, his attention on me rather than her.

"Do you know who might have killed your friend?" I asked.

"I have a few suspicions," said the vampire. "Steve's quest to find the murderer in here is likely to be a disappointment. The killer will have left immediately after poisoning the blood."

"He shouldn't be allowed to distress the patients," said Alissa, her hands clenching at her sides.

Vincent tilted his head. "It sounds like the nurses are winning the argument."

The noise from the corridor was too jumbled for me to make much sense out of it, but having enhanced senses must come in handy.

"Is Steve scared of vampires?" I asked. "Why, it's not like your fangs can bite through stone... can they?"

He gave me a wide humourless smile, and I wished I'd never asked.

"I would advise you to go home, Blair."

Vincent disappeared before I could ask whether he'd

been the one to lure Sky here. I'd say yes, unless my cat was psychic. You never knew.

The important thing was that Alissa and I were free— at least, for now.

"We should go," I said to her. "I know you're meant to be working, but—"

"Yeah." She nodded. "I just hate the thought of Steve rampaging around terrorising the patients. He should be supervised."

"He should, but not by us. If he suspects either of us, the other is guilty by association."

Not to mention her relationship with Bryan of the werewolf pack. How had the gargoyles even known that? Steve might be the leader of the local law enforcement, but he wasn't the most observant person and was prone to rash actions. Like the time he'd arrested me and several other innocent people when Mr Falconer had faked his own death. I had my doubts about his ability to catch the actual killer even if they were sitting in this very room. The vampire was probably better at sniffing out killers.

"If anything, Vincent should be the leader of the law enforcement," I said, as we left the hospital. "There's no way to hide your thoughts from someone."

"You can sense lies," she reminded me. "That's just as useful."

"Not if I don't ask the right questions." Not to mention my ability had been temporarily switched off by a siren's magic recently... a weakness I hadn't been aware of before, and which made me uncomfortable to say the least. I'd begun to grow more secure in my ability to detect whether or not people were telling the truth, but despite using said ability to solve two murders, Steve remained opposed to the idea that I might have anything remotely useful to say. And if the killer wasn't in the room and it was too dark to search outside, I was most definitely not expert enough to solve this particular case.

It was probably for the best that I didn't get involved in yet another murder, but worry for Alissa preyed on my mind. Not to mention, if even Steve was afraid of vampires, who would have the audacity to murder one of them in such a way that it couldn't be passed off as an accident?

"Are you working this weekend?" I asked Alissa.

"Tomorrow. I hope they'll have caught the killer by then, for the sake of the patients."

"Same here. That Vincent, though—he can read anyone's mind. As soon as the killer goes near him, it's over."

"That's why I don't understand how it happened in the first place," she said. "The vampire who died, he had the same ability. He'd have known if the killer was in the room. It's the reason they're so tough to kill. They can see you coming a mile off, through their senses if not through reading your mind. They say stakes are the best way to kill a vampire, but that isn't true."

"Poison, though?" I said. "What type?"

"Hemlock." She grimaced. "Deadly to humans, too. But obviously, the blood in that area of the hospital is reserved for vampires only. They're very picky, for creatures whose diets consist only of blood."

"Sounds like fun for the person who has to deal with it."

"That would be me. Earlier. That's why they thought I

put the poison in there. But I wasn't the only person to go into that room, and besides, they had nothing on me."

"I'm sorry that happened," I said. "And I thought I was the one who kept wandering into murder sites."

Her brow furrowed. "Yes, you do. You shouldn't have come."

"Sky insisted. I didn't actually know you were in handcuffs when he dragged me outside. He and Vincent are friends, after all, so maybe he found out that way."

She shook her head. "There's no way I'll be able to come with you to the falls tonight. They might arrest both of us."

"I have to go," I said. "I know it's dangerous, but—it's my family. I'll be fine. I faced off against killer plants once, remember?"

She didn't smile. "Blair, I really don't think… the falls are dangerous even when it's light outside. Let alone with a killer on the loose. Won't you consider saving it for another night?"

I released a breath. "I don't know how to contact whoever left the note. It might be my only chance." However unappealing the idea of going to the falls alone with a killer wandering around might be. Self-preservation fought curiosity, and self-preservation was on the winning side. But if my family could leave a note, they might at least have signed it. I didn't even know *who* had left it.

My phone rang. Nathan. *Oh no. I guess he heard.*

"Hey," I said to him. "Did you hear? I guess you're on security duty, right?"

"Yes, I am, but I wanted to warn you not to go out tonight," Nathan said. "I found a body in the woods, the police are involved—I know you like your night time excursions, but I guessed you wanted to cut our date short for a reason."

Busted. In fairness, he had a point, but... *who else died?* "A body? Whose?" Not another vampire?

"Don't come out tonight," he repeated.

He hung up. I stared at the phone. "He can't leave me hanging like that."

"Nathan figured out your plan?" she asked.

"No, he still doesn't know. And—and he found a body in the woods. What if it was the person I was supposed to meet with?"

"That's a stretch. I wouldn't jump to that conclusion. They wanted to meet you at the waterfall, not in the forest."

"The forest is right next to the waterfall."

"Blair..." She hesitated. "Wait until morning. You know it's probably nothing to do with you."

The meeting is. I held my tongue. She'd been through enough tonight already, and I still hadn't decided whether or not to go ahead and follow the note's instructions even before dead bodies had started showing up.

I'd nearly paid for my last spate of reckless decisions with my life.

I hope I don't regret this.

3

I was flying. Wings spread wide, over an endless expanse of blue. The wind whipped my hair back and roared in my ears. There were others around me, but my gaze was tied to the sky and I couldn't look away to see who else was there. Under the wind, voices clashed around me, a jumble of noise.

Something was chasing us...

Crash.

For a brief instant, I thought I'd actually hit a tree head-first. Then I blinked dazedly, wriggling upright to find my legs tangled in my bedcovers on the floor. Sky the cat sat where I'd been lying, until he'd nudged me off the bed.

I groaned and disentangled myself from the covers. "Ow. Thanks for that."

"Miaow." Sky sat expectantly on the bed, wearing his 'pet me' expression.

"Yes, I know you warned me about Alissa." I tossed the covers aside. I'd barely slept, knowing I'd made the sensible decision to stay put, but unable to rid myself of a deep, horrible ache in my chest.

I'd missed my chance to meet my family.

But what choice did I have? The forest had been right next to the waterfall, and Nathan's strained voice when he'd told me about the body betrayed panic. Even if my family hadn't been involved in whatever had taken place in the forest last night, they'd probably expected me to stay away from the falls for my own safety.

As midnight passed, I'd looked out the window at the pitch-black garden, wishing there was a way to get a message through to my family. Once or twice I'd been sure I'd seen the flutter of wings, and even grabbed my slippers and ran outside, but found nothing. Just my imagination.

It was way too early to be up on a Saturday, but I had to do something besides lie in bed feeling sorry for myself. Now daylight was here, it was past time for me to find out who'd died in the forest.

I shoved clothes on without really paying attention and half ran from the house, in the direction of the police station. Alissa would not be thrilled at being left behind, but she was the one who'd almost been arrested this time. I wouldn't let anyone else take the fall for my curiosity.

To say the town's prison wasn't my favourite place was an understatement. I didn't have a clue where they took dead bodies, since where vampires and zombies were concerned, not everything *stayed* dead, but in the case of a murder investigation, the police station would be the likely place to find out the details. Despite my rest-free slumber, it'd been seven hours or so since the murder, so maybe they'd still be here.

Sure enough, voices greeted me as I pushed open the door to the brick building where the gargoyles ran the local law enforcement. It appeared to have been built for regular-sized humans, and everything from the low ceilings to the furniture was undersized. Unless they just liked feeling big and important. Who knew.

I looked around, and saw another door open on the left. The huge shape of a gargoyle filled the room, next to—

Nathan turned around with his eyebrows raised. "Blair?"

"I…" Had not rehearsed my excuses. "Alissa got accused of murder," I blurted. "A vampire died at the hospital. So I thought it might be the same killer, or…" My gaze snagged on the table inside the room. "The body is in there?"

"Yes, it is. I spent last night searching the forest for others." He looked like he had, too, judging by the rough stubble on his jaw and the dark circles under his eyes.

"Who is it?" I asked.

"An elf."

No.

It's not your family. Elves might be related to fairies, but I wasn't one. Still…

"How?" I whispered. "A werewolf?" I'd heard their territories were close enough that they sometimes got into scuffles.

He shook his head. "It's not a werewolf kill."

"What are you doing here?" demanded Steve the gargoyle. "Interfering again."

I held up my hands. "I just wanted to see if there'd been any developments on the vampire murder. I'd rather avoid my friend or me facing any other accusations."

"Vampire murder?" Nathan asked. "Who?"

Before I could explain, Steve stepped towards me, unintentionally revealing the view of the room behind me. I made the mistake of looking at the body on the table, and gagged. Luckily, Steve didn't get in my way as I ran outside and threw up in the nearest bush.

Nathan's hand rested on my shoulder. His tone was gentle when he said, "I think you should go home, Blair."

I squeezed my eyes shut. "Alissa was accused of murdering a vampire in the hospital yesterday. At the same time as the attack in the forest, more or less."

"Really? Are you sure?"

I straightened upright, nodding. "He was poisoned. So obviously, no connection there. Maybe it's a coincidence. But Steve nearly dragged both of us in. I didn't even do anything this time."

"You were at the hospital last night, though?" he asked.

He really did make it impossible to make excuses. "I went after Alissa when Sky—my cat—insisted on it. You know what he's like. Anyway, she's off the hook for now, but when you said you found a body, I freaked out. I thought there might be a connection."

"To a poisoned vampire?" he asked. "That's not my area at all, but I can ask at the police if they'd be willing to share any details with me. Just in the interests of keeping you and your friend safe. Don't get any ideas."

"Yeah, right. I'm not the retired hunter here."

His expression darkened. "Maybe not retired for long. That kill doesn't look like it belongs to anyone or anything known to live here."

My stomach turned over and I nearly threw up again. "Seriously?"

"I don't want to alarm you with the details."

I folded my arms across my chest. "I can handle it. As long as I don't have to look at…" I vaguely gestured at the police station again. "Whereabouts in the forest did it happen? Who was it?"

"We've yet to find out. The elves haven't responded to our request for their help with identifying the body."

That was bound to go over well. The elves didn't like the witches, but I wasn't sure where the gargoyles ranked. Surely they all obeyed the laws if they were allowed to stay in the town. "But—was it near the witches' part of the forest?"

"It was on the boundary between elf and witch territories."

Not near the waterfall, then. The shifters occupied the northern part of the forest. The witches, the south. And the elves, the west. I didn't know the exact boundaries, because while the parts of the forest that weren't the witches' weren't exactly forbidden to the rest of us, the shifters and elves were both fairly territorial. That made walking near their territory risky at best, but the falls were neutral territory. Now, with the forest dangerous, I doubted my absent family members would invite me for a second meeting.

But if there was a killer in the forest, Nathan himself had had a narrow escape. "Did they make you search the whole forest last night when whatever killed that elf was still out there?"

"I volunteered to," he said. "It was my job, remember? I

know the forest backwards, even in the dark. But I found nothing. No footprints or traces."

A chill raced down my spine. "No traces at all?"

"I'll go back to search later. I'm helping to identify the possible cause of death. I know most monster-related injuries."

"I can imagine." Actually, I didn't *want* to imagine. Why couldn't I have fallen for a guy with a normal job, like an accountant, or...

Wait. Fallen for? Nope. I wouldn't go that far. Especially with all the secrets I was keeping.

"You don't know what might have killed him, at all?" I asked.

"No."

Lie.

My whole body stiffened. In all the time we'd known each other, my inner lie detector had never gone off around Nathan before. But he was entitled to keep his own secrets, right?

"Go home," he repeated. "I'd try to enjoy the rest of your weekend, so you can be ready for your classes next week. Don't get any more involved in this than you have to."

I squashed my instinct to tell him not to order me around. The murders were none of my business, and I doubted the police would come after Alissa again when Madame Grey found out. She was fiercely overprotective of her grandchildren.

But what can I do? I'd come close to being accused myself. But I was probably the only person in town who knew there was a fairy of some unknown type in the forest last night.

I'd lived here for only a few months, but I'd come to feel Fairy Falls was safe. And logically, the not-so-retired paranormal hunter was absolutely the person to deal with any threats. But I didn't want the guy I was crushing on to end up getting eaten by a monster. That was reasonable enough.

As for the vampire's killer, Sky had only warned me because Alissa was in trouble. That was all.

———

I got back to the flat and found Alissa sitting at the kitchen table. I was still shaky from my experience at the police station, so I made a mug of tea with an infusion of a calming draught, and sat down opposite her.

"Please tell me you weren't where I think you were," she said.

"I went to the police station to check on Nathan. He was up all night dealing with the…"

"Dead body? Who was it?"

"An elf," I said, dropping my gaze to my mug to avoid seeing her shocked expression. "No clue if it has anything to do with whoever killed the vampire, but they're marking it as a wild animal attack. Anyway, have you spoken to your grandmother?"

She nodded. "Yeah. It's safe to say I'm off the hook for now. But… the wolves aren't."

I raised an eyebrow. "What, they're accusing the werewolves? Were there even any wolves in the hospital at the time?"

"I don't know, but you know the rivalry there."

Did I ever. During my first week in town, Vincent had

given me his card, implying I wanted to pick him over the werewolves, and that I could only choose to be an ally to one and not the other. Of course, it didn't help matters that I'd ticked off the leader of the werewolf pack when his beloved daughter had got stuck in her wolf form due to an accident at Dritch & Co. My former co-worker Blythe had been responsible, but since I'd wound up at the centre of that particular incident and I hadn't spoken to anyone from the pack since, they probably still held a grudge.

"There's another issue," Alissa said. "They want me to talk to my ex. To Bryan."

"What, they think *he* did it?"

Heat crept to her face. "I don't know what they think, to be honest, but they think I'm the best person to talk to the pack. Or Steve still thinks I'm guilty and wants to keep me involved without angering my grandmother."

I winced. "They won't be at the New Moon, at least."

"No, he'll be at his house, which means dealing with him trying to lure me inside. Will you…"

"Come with you for moral support? Absolutely."

Not least because I needed to get the wild animal attack off my mind.

"Why accuse him?" I asked. "Seems random."

"He came to see me at work last week. He sneaked into the ward without permission, to bring me flowers and tell me he wanted to get back together. Obviously, I told him to get lost. But the vampire died the next day. I don't think he'd poison someone, and I have no idea if the two of them had any history or not, but he's still on the suspect list."

"Oh. He's not likely to react well, is he?"

"No," she admitted. "Better than the chief, though."

Chief Donovan led the pack. We hadn't spoken since he'd yelled at me in the hospital waiting room and insisted it was my fault Callie had been attacked. One of her other relatives had also called Nathan a cold-blooded murderer, too. Nathan himself seemed to get on fine with my co-worker Callie, at least, but there was definitely some unhappy history between him and the rest of the pack. I hadn't asked for the details. Maybe I didn't want to know. He'd already lied to me once. But I'd be a hypocrite to call him out on it, considering the fairy-shaped elephant in the room. Maybe it was for the best that Alissa and I talk to the pack instead.

Alissa and I left to go to the werewolf's house as soon as she was done with breakfast.

"So why was Nathan at the police station?" she asked.

"He found the body." I filled her in on the rest of the details as we walked.

"Wow," she said. "Hell of a Friday night. I don't think the two cases are likely to be connected. There's a fairly big difference between killing a vampire by stealth and a monster attacking someone in the woods."

I swallowed hard. "Is it common for monsters to run around the forest? Nathan implied he's dealt with this kind of thing before."

"He spoke to you about it?"

"He got dragged out of retirement," I said, not taking her up on her suggestive tone. "He did promise to tell me if he learns anything useful, but he's pretty dead set on me not getting involved in this one."

"He knows what you're like," she said. "And for the

record, I agree with him. You've experienced entirely too much danger since moving here."

"I'm worried about you," I countered. "Those cells are horrible. I wouldn't wish it on anyone. Also, when Nathan said he found a body, he didn't say whose it was, so my imagination went crazy. You know I was meant to meet someone by the falls last night. I had to check."

An ache grew in my chest, the same one that had pursued me for the last few weeks since receiving the note, amplified. Maybe I should have flown in on my boots over the lake without going into the forest at all…

Lost in thought, I tripped over nothing and Alissa caught my arm.

"It's a good thing that you didn't try walking down to the falls in the middle of the night," she said. "You can't even walk in a straight line today."

"I'm tired. And distracted."

"Don't worry, you can go home and nap as soon as this is done. We're at the right road." She pointed to the right, past a park next to the woods. "I should have planned what to ask him."

"Bryan shouldn't be in trouble if he didn't do it, right?"

"No, he shouldn't. Usually only the nurses have access to that room. And the vampires. But he did somehow get all the way into the ward, so it's possible nobody was paying attention. We were in the middle of a busy shift, understaffed, and dealing with some difficulties with that drunken elf patient. That's what I'd have had to deal with if I'd stayed last night."

She walked to the door of one of the brick houses, and knocked.

A man with shaggy blond hair answered a moment

later. He looked grumpy and tired, but his eyes brightened at the sight of Alissa. "You changed your mind?"

"No," she said. "I'm here because someone—a vampire —was murdered at the hospital yesterday. The police think you might be involved, so I'm to get the full story from you."

He blinked. "I was there to see you," he said. "That's the truth."

"You honestly thought I'd let you seduce me at work, if at all?" she said. "I was covered in bodily fluids and wrestling a screaming elf into a hospital bed at the time. You didn't even know what time I was working."

His jaw clenched. "I heard about the vampire."

"Yes, that's what I just told you."

"Not just *that* vampire."

Alissa went pink, to my confusion. "That has absolutely nothing to do with my questions. I'm serious—and for the record, I nearly got locked up myself. You need to give me a convincing explanation as to what you were doing in the hospital."

"*Not* murdering anyone."

True. My ability never lied. He wasn't the killer.

I gave a slight nod when Alissa glanced sideways at me. "Just checking," she said. "You know what Steve's like. I figured you'd rather hear it from me."

A smile snapped onto his face. "You're right. Thanks for warning me. Can I make it up to you later?"

"Not happening, Bryan," she said. "We've been through this, and we're just not right for each other. It would help if you could tell me if you saw anything unusual at the hospital yesterday, though."

"No," he said. "I didn't go anywhere near that room."

Lie.

Huh? Why lie about something like that? Maybe because he didn't want to imply he'd been involved... but I already knew he wasn't the killer.

"Then do you know anyone from the pack who had an issue with Lord Goddard?" she asked. "I know this is probably old news, but the first thing anyone thinks of is rivalries, when this type of thing happens."

"How'd he die? You know a werewolf couldn't kill a vamp in combat."

"He was poisoned," I said. "Well, the blood bags were. I don't know if he was the definite target, but it's safe to say the killer was aiming for a vampire. And I can't promise blame won't fall on the pack, at least until we have other options."

"Look, it's probably someone looking for his inheritance," said Bryan. "Didn't you hear? The guy was loaded, which isn't a surprise considering he was a million years old."

"A few hundred," Alissa corrected. "I didn't even know he had a family."

"Yeah, he did, before he turned into a vampire. So if they find his will, they might get the money, the fancy house... everything. But I honestly didn't know the guy."

No lies there... and no real reason to divert the topic back to the hospital. He might have ended up near the room for any reason. For instance, he'd probably got lost trying to find Alissa, or hidden away to stop the other staff or patients from catching him. Given how he'd behaved when we'd run into him at the New Moon pub, it wasn't out of character for him to wander into Alissa's workplace to ask for her back.

We thanked him and left, ignoring his pointed hints that Alissa might want to join him for a run that morning.

"He's definitely not involved?" she asked, after checking he wasn't listening. "At all?"

"I don't think so," I said. "He definitely isn't the killer. But he lied when he said he'd never been near the blood bag room. Of course, there might have been an innocent reason he was there, so I didn't want to push it."

"There's nothing innocent about tailing me to work."

"You know what I mean." I paused. "Er, what did he mean about *not that vampire?*"

"Ah." A moment passed. "Yes. That."

I frowned. "Something you want to tell me? Is there another vampire?"

"It's… nothing to do with the murder. Nothing at all, actually."

True… and not quite true. My inner lie detector didn't go blaring off, but instinct told me she wasn't telling me everything.

"He said you had a boyfriend?" I asked. "Is it true?"

"It's complicated." She chewed on her lower lip. "Okay, there's a guy. He's a young vampire. My age. You know, vamps aren't generally normal humans before they turn. Not the newer ones, anyway, unless they came from outside of the town."

Of course. I'd learnt recently that wizards could be turned into vampires, but fairies couldn't. The bite would kill them.

"There's a patient at the hospital who was bitten fairly recently," she went on. "He used to be a wizard. I've been helping him adjust. Most vampires leave their families after they turn, because it causes friction when they don't age and their families do. There's a reason a lot of vamps are nomadic. The ones living in Fairy Falls have chosen to settle down, but that doesn't mean they don't remember their former lives. And… let's just say Keith is having trouble adjusting. I was helping him."

"But you like him."

Her cheeks turned pink. "He's a newly turned immortal. I'm not an idiot. I know where this is going. And neither of us has made a move."

"Yet."

"Hey."

"I don't judge," I said. "I just cornered the guy I like at a police station and then threw up over a dead body."

She laughed. "You know, that does help."

"I'm an eternal reminder that it's possible to sink lower." I smiled and shook my head. "I'm also supposed to be practising conjuring spells right now. Not running after werewolves. I don't think they have anything to tell us, but might this new vampire know anything?"

"Not likely," she said. "Like I said, Keith is totally new at being a vampire. He spent his whole life training as a wizard and now this."

I blinked. "Wait, does that mean someone from town bit him?"

"He doesn't know who." She heaved out a breath. "Obviously, it's a crime, so that means the vampires will have a mess on their hands if they find out who did it. I have no intention of getting involved in that. I'm just there to help a patient who needs me—which, by the way, is why I have no intention whatsoever of making a move on him at all, if ever, until he's out there in the vampire world."

"Would it be a real stretch to link whoever bit him to the murder?"

"Probably," she said. "Unless the person who bit him also killed his fellow vampire…"

"Or the guy who died was the one biting people without permission?"

She tilted her head. "I know when I'm beaten. Luckily, Keith's allowed visitors. I can bring you in to talk to him, if I get permission. Vamps are generally pretty good witnesses, so it's possible he picked up on something we didn't."

"Right… the enhanced hearing," I said. "Doesn't that mean he might have heard the killer outside the room? Is he close by?"

"Close enough to hear? Yes, but I doubt he knows one set of footsteps from another. He's pretty new at this. Anyway, you get one round of questions and that's it. And if the police are there, we're leaving."

"Of course," I said. "Don't worry. We'll go when it's definitely safe, if you're sure. Not today. We should go to the lake instead. That'll take both our minds off things, right?"

"Not if you go wandering over to the waterfall," she said. "I know you, Blair."

I didn't argue—yet.

However, when we reached the path down to the lake, two large gargoyles blocked our way. "Where are you going?"

"To the lake," Alissa answered.

The gargoyle grunted. "The forest's out of bounds. So are the falls."

"Really?" I said. "But—"

"No exceptions." The gargoyle spread her wings. I got the message, and Alissa and I headed down to the bank instead.

In their shifted forms, the gargoyles looked even more brutish and scary, leathery wings etched against the pale blue sky. If my family had left another note, or a sign of their presence at the falls, I hadn't a hope of getting past the gargoyles to see.

Alissa pulled me into a hug. "I'm sorry you missed your chance. But you know, you have a family. You have me."

I did. But I couldn't help wondering, all the same: had the killer been after my family?

4

At work the following day, my head was emphatically *not* in the right place to deal with clients.

"Hi, Blair," said Callie, the receptionist, when I walked into Dritch & Co's office. "I heard you had an interesting weekend." Her usual perky smile was missing, and she looked about as tired as I felt.

"I guess they found the body near your territory, right?"

She bowed her head. "My dad… let's just say he's being a little overprotective."

I could imagine, given how he'd handled the incident when his daughter had been stuck in her wolf form.

"It'll pass," I said, though frankly I couldn't imagine what might be lurking in the woods that even the wolf shifters were wary of. Didn't *want* to imagine. And the fact that Nathan had to be the one to deal with it had given me another sleepless night. I still hadn't actually heard from him since he'd had to cancel our date. "Did you hear about the vampire, too?"

"Yeah, word reached the pack. I can't imagine who might have killed him."

"You don't mind vampires?" I didn't think so. Callie was pretty laid-back, as far as shifters went.

"No, I think the rivalry is a bit ridiculous," she said. "It started as a territorial issue, but the werewolves have all the territory they need. That said, they're being absolutely absurd about Nathan being on our territory."

Oh no. I should have seen that coming. "What's the issue with the hunters? Do all werewolves hate them? Your cousin accused him of being a murderer when he was ranting at me while you were stuck in wolf form."

"A friend of his was put down by the hunters for breaking the law," she said. "Obviously when a werewolf goes wild… it's bad. They lose control, all reason, and to keep people safe, the hunters are forced to act. It's a thankless job."

"I can't even imagine." And now I was back on Nathan again. Maybe we'd been doomed from the start. A hunter and a paranormal—a weird one with no memory of her own history—wasn't a match made in heaven, and when you added any number of dead bodies into the mix, it was no wonder that we'd never had the chance to have a deep discussion of our histories.

"Anyway, Nathan's fine. I don't see him as a killer. Nor does any sensible werewolf. My cousin isn't one of those, but don't tell him I said that." She winked.

That wrung a laugh out of me. "I won't tell him to his face, don't worry."

I went into the office with my spirits slightly lifted, though Callie's comments on her family had reminded me of my missed opportunity all over again. I shoved those thoughts behind a door and went to deal with today's client list.

Luckily, we had four people in the office once again, now Blythe's replacement had stepped in. Lena, a blond Eastern European woman whose impeccable outfits put mine to shame, had settled in well enough with our unconventional office space. Lizzie sat beside her, her black hair pulled into a braid. Our resident technological expert was the creator of the office's magical coffee machine, which conjured up a motivational coffee when I hit the button. Picking it up, I carried it to my desk.

Meanwhile, there was Bethan, who occupied the desk next to mine. As the daughter of the boss, she'd inherited her multitasking skills as well as her ability to track down information none of the rest of us had any hope of finding. She had several pens sticking out of her fine dark hair and a small mountain of papers on her desk. I moved my chair out of the way of the slightly open drawer under her desk, which seemed to have been fitted with an expansion spell. Textbooks rattled around as she closed it, along with a faint squeaking noise.

"Morning, Blair," she said.

"Hey. What's on for today?"

"The usual. Veronica wants to discuss your progress with magic, by the way."

"Ah." My progress, if you wanted to call it that, was stuck on pause. I'd spent a few hours practising with Alissa by the lake yesterday, but I had too much on my mind to concentrate. "I'm still in basic lessons. And I probably will be for a while."

Right now, my skill level was below that of a five-year-old starting at the witches' academy. Rita had wanted to move me up to taking group classes soon, but I dreaded the idea of anyone being around to witness my shoddy wand-work. The only reason we'd avoided any major accidents was because Rita always cast a shielding spell on herself. And the classroom.

"Oh, and Alissa texted me about her near-miss on Friday night," added Bethan. "You were there, right?"

"Yeah. Bad luck for Alissa. She just happened to be in the wrong place at the wrong time, and Steve would jump to the conclusion that the most innocent-looking person in the room was responsible."

She winced. "Yeah, it's not surprising they let her go. Nobody wants to cross Madame Grey. I'd say another vamp did it and decided to drag everyone into their feud."

"Really?" I asked. We didn't get many vampire clients, probably because 'a job for life' was true in a literal sense for immortals. They were pretty close-knit. "Why would another vampire turn on their friends? They've all known one another a long time." Apart from the new guy, that is.

"Because they're unpredictable and violent, mostly," she said. "Not in an overt way, either. They'll plot revenge for centuries, I heard. Most people think vamps are creepy, but you don't cross one of them if you want to keep your head. My mother isn't keen on them, either."

"I only found out recently that most of them were paranormals before they turned," I admitted. "Wizards."

Bethan nodded, the pens in her hair bobbing up and down. "They would be. Our rules about not biting humans have been around for a while, in addition to the secrecy rules. They have their own law book, and to be honest, they follow it for the most part. I don't know what might have gone wrong."

The new vamp? No, Alissa was far too sensible to date a potential killer. Though she'd made questionable decisions before as far as her dating life was concerned. Bryan being a prime example.

"I heard it might be part of the werewolf-vampire feud," I said quietly.

"Callie doesn't think so," said Lizzie, who'd apparently been listening in. "And the two of you probably ought to avoid ticking off the boss today. She nearly bit my head off when she caught me messing with the coffee machine earlier."

"Noted."

I worked through the list of clients as efficiently as I could in the hopes that Veronica at least wouldn't be able to berate me for being behind. Today didn't involve any cantankerous wand-makers or tetchy unicorn handlers, so by the time my meeting with the boss rolled around, I was more or less on top of things.

I walked through the reception area to the boss's office, and knocked. The door swung inwards, revealing a woman who looked like an older version of Bethan with straight silvery hair, wearing a crisp suit.

"Ah, Blair," she said.

Every time I went into her office, she'd decorated it completely differently. It was disconcerting to walk into a room covered in fluffy kittens, and then enter the next day to find it decked out like a neon-coloured space station. In celebration of the solstice, she'd opted for an outdoorsy theme—sky blue ceiling, green carpet patterned to look like grass, desk set out like a picnic table. Luckily, she'd opted against conjuring rainclouds inside the office to represent the usual weather conditions in the north of England.

I sat down at the picnic table, which looked downright weird with a computer and a tangle of wires on it.

"You wanted to talk to me?" I asked.

"I wanted to check on your progress in your magical lessons. How's it going?"

"I'm learning conjuring spells at the moment." My lack of skill aside, I was at a disadvantage because I was the oldest student and the only non-competent adult witch in town. The others were kept within the confines of the academy, and nobody was allowed to use their wands outside of the school's boundaries until they passed the basic tests. Everywhere else, when you saw a wand, you had a reasonable amount of confidence it wasn't about to explode in your face. Not so much with mine. Wands were sensitive, and the slightest movement could set off a spell if you weren't careful. Mine would be more likely to backfire on me in a crisis than not. It was a blow to the self-esteem, to say the least.

Veronica leaned forwards. "What else have you covered so far?"

I rattled off the list of spells: levitation, colour-changing, locking and unlocking charms.

"And have you started working with the others yet?" she asked.

Not quite. If anything, the other pupils should probably keep a safe distance from me for as long as humanly possible.

"I have another lesson tonight," I said. "I'll see what Rita says."

She had a more realistic idea of my capabilities than anyone else did, but I had a lot to live up to, considering how powerful my mother had apparently been.

"I have a question," I said clumsily.

"Ask away. I did say you can ask me anything."

"Er, do you know if any fairies have ever come here, aside from the elves?" I asked. "I mean, they were here when my mother was, right?"

"Some of them, certainly, but they won't have known her," Veronica said. "If she did pursue a relationship with a fairy, it wasn't someone who lived here. I wasn't here myself at the time, and I didn't know her that well when we were children."

Right—I'd forgotten she and my mother would be the same age, give or take a few years. Veronica hadn't spent all her life in Fairy Falls and had spent a few years travelling the world. She'd been married once, and had changed her surname to Eldritch after the divorce, but I hadn't asked Bethan for any more details than that.

"So you both lived here as children?" I couldn't help asking. "Er, were you in any of the same classes?"

"I don't believe we were in the same classes, but we were at the academy around the same time. She scored highly on her exams, if I remember, but we went our separate ways after we graduated."

Right. That makes sense. I'd been sure the boss would tell me if she'd known my mother, but being acquaintances with Tanith Wildflower was enough for her to be confident that I'd live up to her name. But there was no use comparing myself to her. I'd barely started my training, while my mother had had a witch and wizard as parents and grew up in this world. I might be a little slow, but my lie-sensing ability was almost faultless. Even without a wand, I did have *some* magical skill, if an unconventional one.

"What was her gift?" I asked.

"I believe it was some form of mind-magic," said the boss, tapping her fingers on the desk. "Not all witches and wizards disclose their gift, and she's been gone a long time. I'd ask your mentor if you're curious."

I already had, and even Madame Grey hadn't been absolutely certain. Blythe, my former co-worker, was a distant relation, but I never wanted anything to do with her again. Besides, she was my age, so she'd never have met my mother.

Veronica rose to her feet. "Return to work," she said to me. "And please, Blair, do be careful around the vampires. They're not pleasant people, and always have a hidden agenda."

And there I was, thinking I could get through this meeting without her picking up a hint that I might be interested in finding the vampire's killer.

"Even Vincent?"

"Especially the elders," she said, a wrinkle in her brow. "Nothing good can ever come of tangling with an elder vampire, Blair. Remember that."

I nodded. "Sure. I'll keep away from the elders."

No need to mention my upcoming interview with the town's youngest vampire after work. It was a long shot, considering the only thing he and the victim had in common was being vampires, but it was possible he might have heard something outside the ward that might point to the killer.

———

Rain pelted down, soaking me to the skin in the few minutes it took to walk to the hospital to meet Alissa and the vampire.

"Hey, Blair," said Alissa, peering at me from beneath an umbrella beside the hospital entrance. "Keith is being discharged, so he agreed to come and talk to us somewhere public. Not outside in the rain. Maybe Charms & Caffeine."

"Works for me." Leaving the hospital would make the other staff less suspicious, at least.

When the young vampire joined us, we all headed for Charms & Caffeine. The hip coffee shop was owned by Lizzie's sister, Layla, creator of the motivational instant-coffee machine.

Keith slouched in his seat and looked sadly at the drinks menu. "I'm never going to be able to drink coffee again."

"Never?" I asked, ordering one of my usual blueberry smoothies. Like a lot of places in Fairy Falls, you just had to tap the menu to order rather than walking to the counter, unless you wanted to order something specialist. Like a lucky latte, for instance.

"No." The vampire scowled at the menu. "Everything tastes like ash after the change."

"Sorry," said Alissa. "I didn't think you'd want to have a discussion at the hospital, and I'm starved after my shift."

"It's fine," said the vampire, in tones that suggested it

was most definitely not fine. "I'll get used to it. One day. In a few years."

"You will," she said, with certainty. "I'll help you."

I covered my face with the menu to hide my grin. At least one of them was totally smitten. Not that I blamed her. Keith had one of those faces which suggested he'd been highly attractive *before* he'd been turned into a waxwork model. His attitude, though, would have me looking for a coffin of my own before the end of the week. As it was, I might as well have worn a sign saying 'Third Wheel'. It was a position I was fairly familiar with, considering all my friends from school were married, so I sipped my drink and waited for Keith to stop morosely contemplating people's lattes.

"We were wondering," I said, "if you knew Lord Goddard. The guy who died."

"I didn't know him," said the vampire. "The only thing the two of us have in common is that we were both wizards before being turned. He was hundreds of years older than me."

"You can still use a wand, right?" I asked.

He shook his head. "It doesn't recognise me now I'm undead."

Ah. We'd dealt with a pirate vampire ghost—long story —who'd still been able to use magic, but maybe it was different for ghosts, and some of the more powerful witches and wizards could use magic without a wand.

"So you don't know who bit you?" I sipped my smoothie. "Doesn't that mean there's another criminal at large?"

"Yes, but the vampires will want to catch the person who bit me more than the human police will," he said, his gaze turning mournful as he looked at Alissa digging into a muffin. "Their rules are strict. No biting. Unless there's a rogue on the loose, someone from this town did it." He looked around the cafe, his gaze downcast. While he'd adapted to the physical changes enough to be let out of the hospital, it'd take longer for him to get over the psychological impact of being turned into the living dead. And he was now going to be stuck as part of that society forever. Eternity was a long time.

"Do you think… I mean, how common are criminal vampires?" I asked, of nobody in particular.

"Depends who you ask," Alissa said through a mouthful of muffin. "Objectively—no more than any other paranormals. Probably less, considering how strict their rules are. On the other hand, if you ask one of the shifters, they'll insist that vampires break the laws all the time and don't get caught. Meanwhile, vamps say the same about the shifters."

"I can imagine," I said. "I'm assuming the vamps are looking for the killer? Vincent probably is. He was pretty mad."

"He would be," said Alissa, sipping her drink. "Immortals are close-knit. The older ones, especially."

That didn't surprise me. The small group of elder vampires were old enough to have known one another for centuries. On the other hand, I couldn't even imagine the fortune you could amass over the course of that many years. Whoever inherited the vampire's possessions would be set for life.

"Did they ever find a will, do you know?" I asked.

"They didn't," said the vamp. "Because it looks like he never wrote one. He thought he'd live forever."

"Seriously?" I put my smoothie down. "No plans for any accidents, or…?"

"We're hard to kill." He said this with a hint of bitterness. "You can stake a vampire, but most people would never be able to catch us. We're fast and strong and resilient, our senses are enhanced, and we'd see or sense anyone creeping up on us. And that's not counting the mind-reading."

"Wait—can you do that?"

He shook his head. "Not yet. But I will."

Wow. All the perks of being immortal… except now he'd have to watch his family age and die, and not even magic could undo what'd been done to him. Under his dismal attitude, he might easily be angry enough to kill the person responsible.

"How long have you been in hospital?" I asked him.

"A week," he said. "Just long enough to get used to all the blood. Then I get inducted into vampire society." He didn't sound thrilled at the prospect. "I get some time off now to recover, and I guess one of them then shows up to tell me what to do. Vincent has already visited me every day."

"Wait, he has?"

I supposed as the eldest, he'd have more of an insight into the process, but it'd have been a long time since he went through it.

"I offered to lend an ear," said Alissa.

More than an ear, by the look of things. With some difficulty, I managed to refrain from saying that aloud.

I took another sip of my drink. "Did you see or hear anything odd at the hospital when he died?"

The vampire shook his head. "No. My ward was

nearby, but since he was poisoned, I guess he died quickly. I'm under watch all the time in case my bloodlust goes out of control, so I didn't see when the police showed up."

True—and I probably should have asked Alissa for more details beforehand. If he was being watched, he couldn't have got hold of the poison. Especially if he'd been stuck there for a week.

"Anyway." He gave the menu a last sad look and got to his feet. "I should get home. Tell my parents I'm out of hospital. It'll be awkward, but what isn't awkward about being one of the living dead?"

"I'll see you later," added Alissa. "Let me know if you need anything else, okay?"

"Sure." Keith cast a mournful look around the café, then slouched off.

"He's not wrong," I said, returning my attention to my drink. "That must be a weird conversation to have. *By the way, I'm going to live forever.*"

"No kidding," said Alissa.

"Also, you seriously underplayed the chemistry," I said to her. "You two couldn't have been closer if he'd been sitting in your lap."

"That's my line," she said, her cheeks going pink. "You and Nathan—"

"It's not happening anytime soon, at this rate." I drank the last of my smoothie.

"They still have him running around after monsters?" she asked.

"Yep. He hasn't called or texted, so I assume he's run off his feet." The forest remained under guard, as far as I knew, and so did the falls. As long as they didn't catch the monster, I hadn't a hope of finding out if my family had ever been there.

I definitely shouldn't be thinking about slipping past the gargoyles to have a look, just to see if my relatives had left another clue behind.

Or the murderer.

I shoved the thought aside. It bounced back like a jack-in-the-box.

Alissa's gaze shone with sympathy. "It's his job, right? He has years of experience. He'll be fine, and as soon as it's done, the two of you will become official."

As opposed to becoming one of the undead. Monsters weren't the only threat out there in the woods.

Operation 'don't think about it' was going swimmingly.

"Hmm. Yeah. I guess." I cast about for a change of subject. "Keith, though. I forgot he was under watch all week."

Alissa's mouth pressed together. "It's the reason the police quickly dropped him as a suspect. He doesn't know who bit him, and besides, he can't undo what was done to him. There's no point in holding a grudge, let alone attempting retaliation."

"Don't worry," I said. "I don't think he did it." He might be extremely resentful of his new status as an immortal, but he'd had no access to poison in the hospital, and wouldn't have known who to target. Not knowing who bit him must be tough to deal with, though.

She exhaled in a sigh. "He's not having a great time of it. After he tells his family, he then has to be inducted into the vampires' society while knowing one of them illegally bit him."

"Maybe it wasn't one of them," I said, thinking of the body in the woods. "Maybe… it *was* a rogue. Just how strong is a vampire? I've never seen one in action."

I'd seen Vincent move so fast that he was little more than a blur, but I couldn't imagine him ever being surprised by an attacker. Which made the killer a creative one, if nothing else. It'd be easy, however, for one of them to sneak up on a human and bite them without ever being detected. Even by a wizard.

"Strong," she said. "They can snap a man's neck with their bare hands, but most of them rarely use that strength. If anything, it's a disadvantage. We spent most of the week having to remove things from the ward after he accidentally broke them. And when a vampire flies into a tantrum, it's terrifying. Okay, it's not quite as scary as when a werewolf loses it and shifts, but still. And then there's those enhanced senses of theirs."

"Hmm. Can't one of them sniff out who planted the poison?"

She shook her head. "Like I said—too many people go in and out of that room. And Steve had people charging around all over the place, so they've left their scent all over the hospital. Also, the presence of so much fresh blood tends to dull a vampire's other senses."

"It seems to me that the police are really good at missing clues," I said, checking the time on my phone. I had a lesson with Rita this evening… and I hadn't checked if she'd left me any assignments. "Wouldn't a vampire make a better detective?"

"You'd think so, but they tend to dislike paperwork."

"Speaking of, I just remembered I have homework for

today's lesson." I dug in my bag for my notes. "Reckon I can fill this out in five minutes?"

"Sure you can. Good luck."

I didn't need luck. I needed to grow a magical bone in my body.

5

Rita studied my scribbled notes, her glasses sliding down her nose. "You grasp the theory well."

I tried not to breathe out a sigh of relief. No reason to let on that I'd filled out the worksheet in the five minutes I'd had to spare before I'd had to dash to my lesson. I'd perfected the skill when I'd been a student, but it'd been a while since I'd spent an extended period of time in a classroom.

A redhead who wore an incalculable number of bangles on both her arms, Rita was eccentric but a good teacher. Despite my lacklustre studying skills, our one-to-one classes were pushing my knowledge of the magical world forward with every lesson. Pity my practical abilities had yet to catch up.

Rita put my notes aside. "Right, Blair. It's time to try the colour-changing spell again."

Time for round forty-seven.

I pointed my wand at the cup on my desk and rotated

my wrist. Carefully. The colour-change spell had been the first spell I'd used, accidentally. You'd think that would make it easier for me to use on purpose, but that would be putting too much faith in my capabilities.

A burst of light from my wand's tip hit the wall, turning its surface… liquid.

"Undo!" Rita spun around and pointed her own wand at the wall, and the bookshelves stopped melting. "You were too far to the right. Circle. Like this."

"I don't have a steady hand." I waved the wand again, but the spell missed the cup and hit the desk, which promptly collapsed.

Another wave of her wand repaired it. "Again." She grabbed my arm and guided my motions. Her grip was like steel. I winced, but slowly rotated the wand—

"Hey, I did it!" The cup was purple.

So was the rest of the room.

I lowered my wand. "Maybe I need more than the safety setting."

She waved her wand to undo the spell and pinched the bridge of her nose. "No, you need to learn to apply moderation. Put your wand down and try with this." She passed me the practise stick I'd spent entirely too many hours swirling around in an attempt to learn how to aim a wand properly. Despite the weeks of practise, it wasn't paying off in practical lessons.

Swirl to the right, left, flick. I could do it in my sleep, but when it came to aiming at the right target, my focus levels weren't the greatest. When I was experienced enough, I'd only have to think of a spell and it'd work with a casual flick of my wand. Attempting to slow my racing thoughts was like putting a harness on a unicorn.

Flick. I nearly poked Rita in the eye and stammered an apology. I turned so that my left hand faced towards her instead. *Swirl, left, right—*

The cup turned maroon. I was so startled, my wand slipped from my grip.

Not a wand. The stick.

I gaped at Rita. "Er… was that supposed to happen? Did you do that?"

She shook her head slowly. "No, I didn't."

I stared at the stick, then at my wand, which lay where I'd left it on the desk. Had the spell come from the wand? It'd happened too fast for me to tell. I'd seen Ava cast a spell without a wand, but that level of skill was reserved for advanced witches and wizards only. Without a wand, we weren't necessarily powerless, but I'd thought casting a spell without one required years of study.

"I think we need to ask Madame Grey to turn on your safety setting," Rita said, firmly planting the wand in my hand again. "I will go and discuss the matter with her. You're dismissed early."

Dismissed. I'd worked magic without a wand and ended up chastised for it.

I returned my wand to its case, my cheeks burning with humiliation. What in the world was wrong with me? The wand certainly worked, if in an unorthodox manner, but the circumstances I'd acquired it under meant that it didn't have the same restrictions as other witches' and wizards' wands. What if it was permanently defective? I'd been struggling with the most basic spells for weeks, and now magic had finally worked for me and I couldn't even conjure up so much as an explanation.

Maybe Madame Grey would be able to help. She'd be

in a coven meeting now, so I headed out into the entrance hall to wait for her—and instead found Nathan, standing outside the door to the classroom.

"Hey, Blair," he said.

"Hey," I said. "How's the case going?"

"Not great," he said. "I've just spoken to Madame Grey about upping the town's defences. Unfortunately, that means working with the shifters, and they're less than thrilled about being asked to act as guard dogs. Or wolves."

"Or badgers, foxes..." I cut myself off before I got carried away. "So you're working with them?"

"No, I'm working alone."

"That doesn't seem fair," I said. "You're the only security guard here, so surely they need backup. You can't watch the entire forest at once."

"Oh, I'm not," he said. "The gargoyles are there, too."

"Yeah, but they can't properly fly in the woods, right? And it's not your job to hunt monsters any longer. Is it?" I was genuinely curious.

"No, but I'm liable to be called back into the field at any time," he said. "My whole family is in the business, so there's no real escape from it."

"I didn't know that." I really should have made an effort to ask more questions. Maybe now was finally the time to admit I wasn't fully human... but how in the world to broach the subject? "Erm, do the others in your family hunt monsters in the area?"

"Not here, but close. They're based in Grasmere."

"Wait, are you saying there have been monsters roaming the Lake District the whole time? Is there a Yeti of Scafell Pike?"

His mouth twitched into a smile. "No yetis. They prefer a less wet climate."

I didn't even know if he was joking or not. At least I'd improved his mood, in preparation for the bombshell I was about to drop. "Actually, there's something I have to tell you. I—"

The door slammed open and a vampire ran in, so quickly that he collided headfirst with a pillar.

Nathan ran towards him. "What is it? You're bleeding."

"Lord Goddard's blasted house," said the vampire. "I need a witch or wizard to help me undo the wards."

"Er, I'm a witch," I said. "What kind of wards are we talking about? Is it to do with his inheritance?"

I felt Nathan's eyes on me, but I'd explain how I knew later.

"You might say that," said the vampire. "That paranoid fool left defences on his house that none of us has been able to penetrate. I think they require a witch or wizard to break in."

"I'm still learning, but…" I looked behind me at the door to Madame Grey's office. "I can ask someone to help you."

I knocked on the door. A moment later, Madame Grey herself answered. A tall woman dressed in grey to match her name, with white hair grown past her shoulders, she looked me up and down through a pair of silver-rimmed spectacles. "Blair? What is it?"

"Trouble," I said. "Vampire-related trouble."

———

The vampires lived—or unlived—up to their reputation. They stood like particularly loud wax statues, arguing with one another. Several were bleeding from trying to get into Lord Goddard's house, but they'd persisted until it became clear all the ways into the house were protected by magical defensive wards.

Madame Grey hadn't been able to get any other witches to volunteer to help her, which left me to go along as her temporary assistant. Not that I'd pass up an opportunity to see whatever Lord Goddard had wanted to protect so badly. As a bonus, I had Nathan at my side, keeping an eye out for trouble at Madame Grey's request.

"How are you holding up, Blair?" he asked, as Madame Grey left me awkwardly holding her props while she went to set up a spell around the house's perimeter. The entire building was covered in wards, and she was now on round three of unlocking spells after the first two had failed.

"Not too bad. He was one paranoid vampire."

"It makes sense, given how long he lived," Nathan said. "They're difficult to kill, but that doesn't lessen the paranoia."

I tilted my head. "Have you ever killed one?"

"You're asking me delicate questions in front of people with enhanced hearing again."

"Oops. Sorry."

The vampires seemed more interested in debating over who was going to get the inheritance. There was a rumour of a solid gold coffin, which struck me as a bit excessive. Being next to Nathan gave me a level of comfort I couldn't deny, though now he'd reminded me everyone would be able to hear what we said no matter how quietly we spoke, this wasn't the time to tell him about my fairy family. Yet.

Madame Grey returned to the front of the house. Despite the mud from the recent rain, she must have doctored her long coat with a spell that stopped her from getting any on her, which was more than I could say for the state of my boots.

"The wards seem to be designed to be activated by the owner only," she said, beckoning me over again. "However, Lord Goddard did not consult the coven before setting them up. I believe they may work for his living relatives, but nobody else, not even me."

Grumbles came from the vampires. Of course, none of them was related to him, so they wouldn't actually know his living relatives.

"Why can't we just walk in?" asked one of the vampires. "Where's the will?"

"The will is likely inside the house," she said. "Did any of you visit him while he was alive?"

"Yes, a few times," one of the vampires said. "But there weren't any visible defences then."

"The wards must have been set to come on after he expired," Madame Grey said. "If he ever expected to."

Lucky Keith the newbie vamp wasn't around to witness this major crash course in the disadvantages of being one of the undead.

Vincent stood overlooking the other vampires from a distance, wearing an expression of abject boredom. I didn't quite have the courage to walk over and start questioning him, not with everyone on edge. So much for my promise to the boss to stay away from the elders.

"Is there no other way around it other than asking his

relatives?" I asked Madame Grey. "What type of ward is it?"

"This is a shielding spell." She examined the gate. "No exceptions."

"That's not fair," said one of the vampires. "We knew him for hundreds of years. He didn't even have any human friends."

"This ward is set to react to his blood, specifically," observed Madame Grey. "It's likely a distant relation will be enough."

"Is that why it cut us?" asked one of the vampires.

"I imagine so," she said. "This is not a matter for the covens, however. You're to make arrangements for meeting his family as you see fit."

Nobody dared argue with her. Instead, they went for the nearest witch—me. "Why do the wizards get first pick? That's not fair."

"Hey, I didn't know the guy," I said. "I'm no relation at all. I don't know his family, either."

Nathan stepped in front of me. "That's enough. We're leaving."

"Yes, we are," I said, as though his protective tone hadn't warmed me all over. Oh, boy.

Grumbling followed us as we turned and left. So many defences, and nobody could breach them. Was it a simple security issue, or was there something in there that Lord Goddard didn't want anyone to find?

"He thought he'd live forever," I muttered to Nathan. "Seems like he got cocky. Unless he pulled a Mr Falconer and faked his death."

"No, he's dead, all right," Nathan said darkly. "I asked for the reports from the hospital. If this is likely to be a recurring issue, the hospital is going to have to take steps, too."

"You think there's someone out there trying to bump off vampires?" I asked, dropping my voice. "Unless every single one of them has the same level of paranoia, it looks like he was targeted on purpose."

"Perhaps, but the way they went about it seems fairly inefficient. How would the killer know he would go into the blood donations room at that particular moment in time?"

"I guess it seems unlikely," I admitted. "They don't have a ton of security around the room, though. Vampires just walk in and out all the time."

"Precisely," he said. "They've had to schedule staff to cover that corridor, but I might be called in there later."

"I don't know how they expect you to search the forest as well. You're only one person. They really need to hire more security." At this rate, we'd get another date in about a year.

"We both have full schedules," he said, as though he'd read my mind. "Are you free on Friday night? I'm not scheduled to go to the forest until late evening, so I have time to see you for a bit."

"Yes," I said, probably too enthusiastically. But it was worth it when he beamed at me. "I'm free that evening."

"Good. I can walk you to the end of your road, but I need to go and report to the police station again."

"Sure." It wasn't dark yet, nor was it raining again, but the idea of him going into the forest alone sent nervous flutters through my chest, almost as much as the idea of another date. Maybe this time I'd actually get to kiss him. He'd been positively gentlemanly the whole time we'd been together, not overstepping any boundaries, yet I couldn't help wondering if he expected *me* to make the first move.

Building up my hopes for our next date might end in another monster attack, so I attempted to set my excitement levels to 'realistic', and walked the rest of the way home alone.

"What's up?" asked Alissa, looking up as I walked into the living room. "Did you and Nathan have fun?"

"We had a blast," I said. "Nothing like watching vampires walk into the wards around Lord Goddard's house like dogs trying to walk through a glass door. They kept getting hit by the wards until Madame Grey told them to cut it out. Someone really didn't want anyone getting hold of his treasure."

Alissa lifted her head. "Treasure? Like actual buried treasure, or…"

"A solid gold coffin, apparently." The cats had taken over the rest of the sofa, so I sat in the armchair. "I think that's probably nonsense, though. They're working themselves into a frenzy over nothing."

"Does Nathan have any more ideas?" asked Alissa.

"He thinks Lord Goddard was targeted at random," I said. "And that the killer was aiming for a vampire—any vampire. The method they used wasn't efficient enough for them to guarantee they'd get the right target."

Her eyes widened. "That's why the hospital upped security, right? They think it might happen again."

"Possibly," I said. "I don't know if I agree with him or not. Lord Goddard did seem to think someone was out to get him, if the state of his house is anything to go by."

"If he knew he was going to die, wouldn't he have left

instructions on how to get his inheritance somewhere?" she asked.

"I don't think he did know," I said, "but it doesn't mean he didn't have enemies. I heard about vampire rivalries, and then there's the pack… not that I think they did it," I added hastily. "But when you add in those weird animal attacks in the forest, I can't help feeling that there's something here in Fairy Falls that shouldn't be."

And that it might be linked, however tentatively, to whoever had left me the note.

6

The rest of the week passed without any more vampire-related trouble, and no news came of either the murderer or the beast in the forest.

I was still banned from practical magic lessons until I got my wand under control, so I spent my sessions doing theory work, keeping my head down and staying out of trouble. At least until Friday, when Alissa rang me when I was leaving work.

I pulled out my phone. "Hey, Alissa."

"Hey, Blair," she said, her voice muffled. "They've called me in for questioning at the hospital again."

"Again? *Why?*"

"Everyone who was on shift when the murder happened has been ordered to come for another grilling from Steve and his band of stony friends."

"Are you on your way there now?"

"Yes, but Blair, I don't want you getting into trouble as well. You know Steve's a nasty piece of work."

"He's a bully." I picked up speed, readjusting my

shoulder bag. "I'm not on the suspect list this time so he can't argue with me for coming to show you moral support. And I won't let him lock you in jail."

"I'm not going to win this one, am I?" said Alissa.

"Nope. If he wants to accuse my friends, he gets to put up with me being a nuisance," I said. "Also, a vampire literally read your mind and knew you weren't guilty. Steve has to expect a backlash if he goes around accusing the same people all over again."

"It's possible the vampires missed something," she said, though she sounded as doubtful as I felt. "Mind-reading isn't always a hundred percent accurate. They can't read every thought in every person's head."

"Vincent said he gets flashes of what I'm thinking when I'm… emotional," I admitted, turning into the high street. "Agitated, he said. If the killer was calm, he might have gone by unnoticed. Also, can vampires block one another from reading each other's minds?"

"Haven't a clue," said Alissa. "That's why it's absurd that they're accusing me at all. I'm not an expert on vampires, either. When I was at school, vamps weren't really covered in our education beyond the basics. They probably didn't want to give a bunch of teenage witches and wizards any ideas."

"I've never seen a teenage vampire," I said. "Guess it's down to the rules about not biting people. Also, they don't age, so it's probably for the best that if they're going to turn, they do so as adults."

"Yeah, there's complicated rules. If you want to turn, you have to go and appeal to their leader. Vincent, in this case."

I grimaced. "Yeah, no thanks. It doesn't strike me as

something anyone signs up for voluntarily."

Certainly not Keith, anyway.

"No. I'm in the waiting room now. They're going to call me in soon."

"I'll be there in a minute." I ended the call and hurried the rest of the way down the road to the hospital.

What was Steve playing at? The murder had been long enough ago that the killer might be halfway across the country by now. Several gargoyles had gathered outside the hospital, and glowered at me when I reached them.

"Where are you going?" asked the stocky female gargoyle I'd spoken to a couple of times before. She wasn't quite as tetchy as Steve, but that wasn't saying much.

"To meet my friend," I said. "Come on, you know *I'm* not the killer."

"You're a menace," she said.

As several people exited the hospital, I seized my chance and darted past the gargoyles into the reception area. Grumbles followed me, but they didn't kick up a fuss and haul me out.

Alissa was nowhere in sight, and nor was Steve, which must mean she was being questioned in one of the offices. Pairs of gargoyles blocked all the exits from the waiting room.

Not your best plan, Blair. Had they decided to repeat the questionings because they thought the killer would target someone else? It seemed the logical solution, given that the murderer wouldn't have known for certain that Lord Goddard would be the one to drink the poisoned blood, but there was nothing remotely logical about re-questioning people who'd already been proven a hundred percent innocent. It was probably Steve flexing his muscles and trying to prove that he was actually getting somewhere in the investigation.

"I don't believe you're one of the suspects," said Vincent's voice from beside my shoulder.

Someday, I'd learn not to jump when he appeared behind me. "I'm here to support a friend."

"Madame Grey's granddaughter," he said. "Yes, she spent some time with our newest recruit."

I twisted around to face him, so I wouldn't have to listen to him creepily speaking into my ear. "You're working on inducting him into vampire society?"

"I suppose you might say that. He's learning. Your friend, however, needs to learn that her path will only end in heartbreak."

"Er, you should probably be telling her that, not me."

"Are you quite certain?"

I opened my mouth, then closed it. Was he warning me about Nathan? *He's not the type of person you need to ask for advice on romance from, Blair.* Then again, since he'd lived long enough to have doubtless experienced heartbreak at least once, maybe he was.

"I have no intention of invading your privacy, Blair. I rarely feel the need to pick specific thoughts from people's minds."

"You can do that?" I seized the chance to ask what I'd been wondering earlier. "So you can control it? The mind-reading?"

"To some extent, but vampires are hard-wired to see everyone as an enemy. I usually cast a brief net over everyone present when I enter a room in case anyone has nefarious intentions."

That sounded exhausting, to be honest. Not to

mention *he* was the one who looked like he had nefarious intentions. "So it's unusual that someone managed to kill Lord Goddard. Did he have enemies?"

"We all do."

"Have you questioned the other vampires?"

"No," he said. "It would be seen as a challenge. Vampires cannot enter one another's property without an invitation. The same rule extends to anybody's home, in fact."

I blinked. "What? Really?" I vaguely remembered something similar from when I'd studied Dracula at school, but I'd thought modern vampires were different.

"It's considered a courtesy."

"Is that why none of the vampires can get into his house? Aside from the wards?"

He tilted his head. "He must have set them up before he was turned, I imagine. Quite the dilemma."

"I was under the impression everyone was off to hassle his wizard family instead, since they're probably the ones who get the inheritance."

He sniffed. "I have no interest in the matter of the inheritance. I care only for bringing down whoever has decided to target my fellow vampires." The merest hint of danger entered his voice, giving me the pressing need to back away.

"You think they'll attack again?" I asked warily.

"There is something here that shouldn't be." His voice was soft, quiet, yet somehow terrifying.

I cast a brief gaze around the waiting room, from the gargoyles in the corridor to the nurses gathered in a huddle, giving the gargoyles the occasional glare. "What, in here?"

"No," he said. "In the town. I smell it in the air."

Since he had enhanced vampire senses, I was inclined to believe him. "Er... can you be a little more specific? What's in town that shouldn't be? Have you told the other residents?"

"I cannot say I know what it is, only that it shouldn't be here."

That wasn't cryptic at all. Vampires. Shaking my head, I looked up to see the door to one of the rooms open, and Alissa walked out.

The vampire was gone in an instant, a breeze stirring my hair in the wake of his sudden departure. "Hey," I said to Alissa. "Did it go okay?"

"Yeah. He's still being all touchy, but he's like that with everyone. I'm not too worried. Were you talking to Vincent again?"

"Yep. He thinks there's something in town that shouldn't be."

Her brows rose. "Like what?"

"Haven't a clue. Vampires are pretty tuned into things, though, considering they can sniff out an enemy a mile off." Not that the vampires seemed keen to throw themselves into harm's way—with the exception of the ever-persistent vampires trying to break through Lord Goddard's magical wards.

"Did he tell you anything else?" she asked.

"Only that he can turn the mind-reading on and off on command, but if anything, that makes it even *more* creepy."

I decided not to tell her what he'd said about her relationship with Keith being doomed to lead to heartbreak. It wasn't my place, and heaven knew I was making enough potentially disastrous errors in my own relationship.

On cue, a text from Nathan showed up. Date cancelled, courtesy of Steve the Spoilsport insisting that he take over from one of the gargoyles guarding the forest. At this rate, we'd get another date after I passed my wand exam, which looked about as likely as Vincent taking up tap dancing.

———

The doorbell rang early the following morning. Since it was a Saturday, I assumed someone else had an early visitor. Then a knocking came at the flat door. Alissa groaned, while I scrambled around looking for some clothes, highly regretting that last witch cocktail. Alissa and I had gone out for drinks last night, and after consuming enough cocktails, it turned out their hangover-repellent wore off. Swilling a glass of water, I winced as the doorbell rang again. Alissa didn't stir, so it was on me to see who wanted to speak to us at this hour in the morning.

"Miaow." Sky wove through the living room and wrapped himself around my legs.

"You're clingy today." I stroked him one-handedly, and detached him from my ankle to go and answer the door. Sky's indignant yowling followed me across the room.

I expected a delivery or a new vampire-related surprise. Instead, Nathan stood on the doorstep, his dark hair curling into eyes shadowed with sleeplessness.

"Nathan?" I said, wishing I'd had a proper shower.

"What're you doing here? I thought you were on guard duty."

"Actually," said Nathan, "I've been called in to talk to a vampire on behalf of the police. He asked to speak to you."

My heart jumped into my throat. "Me? Why?"

"He says you know Vincent." His voice held a questioning undercurrent.

"I wouldn't say we know one another particularly well," I said. "He's friends with my cat. I did speak to him at the hospital yesterday while I was waiting for Alissa to get out of Steve's latest interrogation. Has he been telling the people I'm the vampire whisperer?"

"Vincent told this vampire, Lord Anderson, that you were the person to speak to," he said. "Understandably, some paranormals are reluctant to speak to a hunter alone, even a retired one."

An uneasy feeling stirred. Sure, I know what Nathan had had to do as a hunter. I could read between the lines even if a werewolf hadn't yelled it in my face a few weeks ago, but it wasn't something I wanted to think about while fighting a hangover and up to my neck in murders.

The real question: did I feel safer with him or a vampire? No contest there.

"Okay, I'll come." I was kind of curious as to what this vampire wanted to share with me instead of meeting with the police. Vincent hadn't told anyone about my lie-sensing abilities, right?

"Good," said Nathan. "I didn't want to impose on you, but he's being quite insistent about it."

"Weird. I've never spoken to a vampire aside from Vincent, and I wouldn't say we were close." He'd read my thoughts—maybe the intimate ones—but honestly, the same was true of any vampire who stepped near me, and he'd likely done the same to half the town. No, it was my little fluffball of a familiar who was, once again, responsible for dragging me into vampire drama. "I'm going to feed my cat, then we'll go."

I found the cat in question sulking on the sofa, and he didn't even look up when I tipped some food into his bowl.

"Sorry I shut you in." I walked to the sofa to give Sky a stroke. "Why are you trying to push me into befriending the vampires?"

"Miaow." Sky huffed and turned his head away.

"I'll see you later. Maybe let me know in advance if you want me to play vampire whisperer next time?"

"Can you not communicate with him yet?" Nathan asked, as I re-joined him at the door.

"Oh, he can, but he's pretty selective with what he shares," I said. "I bet he's the one who's been going around making friends with the vampires. He and Vincent are buddies, but I guess vampires don't have familiars."

"He picked you," Nathan said. "As far as the rules go, that makes him your familiar."

"Yep." I checked the door was locked. The cool breeze soothed my headache and made me feel a little more awake. "I also think he's somehow communicating with the vampires. Like, psychically. I never asked Vincent if vampires can read animals' minds as well as humans', but familiars are different."

He nodded, a frown puckering his brow. "You heard from Vincent?"

"Yesterday, when Alissa was being questioned at the hospital. I guess he was on the list for questioning, too," I said. "Anyway, he said that vampires' mind-reading skills are pretty extensive. He can scan everyone in a room in a few seconds. Which means he'd know if anyone he'd encountered in town was the killer. And as I said, everyone in the hospital is pretty much accounted for. I think an outsider did it, and so does Vincent. Do the police think the other vampires might be involved?"

"No," he said. "They don't like the idea that one of them might have turned on their fellow vampire, but Lord Anderson roused their suspicions because he and Lord Goddard had an ongoing feud. For centuries."

"That sounds tiring, to be honest."

"You're not the grudge-holding type?" he queried.

"Nope. With one exception—Blythe," I admitted. "It's not really a grudge. It's more like I know that whenever I run into her, she'll start messing with me. Like when she showed up at our last date."

"I forgot about that," he said. "She's not still making trouble for you?"

I shook my head. I hadn't seen her since then, and now I thought about it, I wasn't sure Nathan actually knew we might be related.

We reached a grand old house, which I'd come to expect of the vampires by now. Balconies, extensive gardens, the works. It was in perfect condition, as though its owner was dedicated to cleaning the place regularly. I hesitated beside the gates in case some defences showed up like the wards on the other vampire's place, but Nathan walked right through without a problem. I followed close behind, wondering what in the world had possessed the vampire to think *I* was the one who could get him off the hook. I did not have a spectacular track record in that department. The only explanation was that he'd somehow heard of my lie-sensing skills. I wasn't sure I liked that. Sure, word would spread beyond the witches eventually, but I still wasn't a hundred percent sure if the ability was from my witch or fairy side. Thanks to the investigation, I'd had no chances to tell Madame Grey I'd inexplicably cast a spell without my wand in my hand, and Rita hadn't given a time frame for when I'd be allowed to take part in practical lessons again. At this rate, probably not until the investigation was over and things were back to normal.

Nathan rang the old-fashioned bell pull. A moment later, the door opened and a vampire appeared on the spot as though he'd been waiting for us the whole time.

While Vincent looked thirty at most, this vampire looked… not exactly his age, but older. More mature. Maybe he'd been middle-aged when he'd turned. I had yet to ask for the details on how that kind of thing worked. His jet-black hair was streaked with grey, and his shoulders stooped a little.

"Hello," Nathan said. "You asked to speak to Blair."

"Uh," I said. "Hi."

"I am Lord Anderson," said the vampire.

"Yes. You wanted to speak to me? Why?"

"I think you know why."

Did vampires take classes in how to speak in that creepy tone? I should ask Alissa if Keith had told her.

"You're being accused of murder, from what I hear," I said. "I'm not sure why you think I'm the person to help you out. Did you and Lord Goddard have some kind of rivalry?"

"I wouldn't kill him," he said. "That'd spoil the fun."

Fun? *Vampires.* "What's fun about spending years bickering with someone?"

"Come back in a few centuries and ask me the same question," he said.

"I'm not a vampire," I pointed out. "You spoke to my cat, didn't you?"

"No, I spoke to Vincent."

That little… he'd known when he spoke to me that the vampire was planning to invite me in to defend him and decided not to give me any warning.

"I'm not… I showed up for my friend because I knew she wasn't the killer. I don't even know you."

"No," he said. "I suppose not. I was curious to meet you."

"Any reason?" Because I was the newbie in town? Or because of my family? Maybe he'd been a wizard before turning, like Lord Goddard had.

"Your ability allows you to sense lies," he said. "So you know I'm not the murderer."

Truth. "Yes, it does. Did Vincent tell you that?" I couldn't recall actually telling him in person, but obviously, he'd plucked it from my thoughts somewhere.

"Yes, he did."

"You do know the police don't care about my ability?" I said to him. "They don't want or need my help and they won't take my word for it. If I tell them you're not the killer, they'd act like I'm just a regular person. It won't help you."

"Is that so?" He paused. "Such a pity. I would wager that the police need you more than you think, Blair Wilkes."

Okay…

"Even if they did," I said, "Steve's head is hard as granite. Literally. He won't bend."

"Maybe there needs to be new blood," he muttered.

What was it with vampires using that expression? "Not my decision," I said firmly. "I'm a witch, I work in paranormal recruitment, and that's about it."

"That's not all there is," he said. "I think you know that."

I froze, acutely conscious of Nathan's presence at my side, and possibly more conscious of the vampire's penetrating stare.

Stop it.

Lord Anderson took a step backwards, to my surprise. "*Very* interesting," he said. "I see Vincent wasn't misinformed on your talents. Good day to you."

And he closed the door, leaving me blinking after him. "What...?"

Nathan turned to me. "What was that about?"

"I..." I gaped at the closed door. "I think I *blocked* him from reading my mind. Or did something while he was in my head. Unless he was faking that reaction."

"How did you know he was doing it?" His tone wasn't accusatory, just curious.

"Vincent has the same look on his face when he reads my mind," I said. "Also, when a vampire spaces out, they're either about to go for the neck, or they're poking their fangs into my thoughts instead."

That got a small smile out of him, but a hint of distrust remained. "I assume he isn't going to explain why he dragged you over here without the police actually being present."

"Yeah, he's not the type to offer an explanation." I shook my head. "Weirdos. The lot of them."

"Do you include Vincent in that?"

"Yes, whatever my cat says." I rolled my eyes. "Honestly. I never really thought another vampire would be responsible for the murder. Poison seems too… cowardly, almost. I guess there might be truth to what Lord Anderson said… about the wizards set to claim his inheritance. I suppose they're being mobbed by vampires now."

"We can find out."

I arched a brow. "Did you suggest we actually get involved?"

His lips twitched. "I know that look on your face, Blair. You're about to use those boots of yours to go snooping."

A flush spread from my neck like sunburn. Maybe he had seen my uncoordinated swooping around the skies after all.

"I would if I knew his relatives' addresses," I admitted. "But they're one online search away. Or I could just fly around until I find whichever house is surrounded by vampires. It's not hard to miss."

"No, I can't imagine it is," he said. "Luckily for both of us, I know the address of Lord Goddard's sole heir—a man named Peter. He's a bachelor and has been hiding from vampires all week. But I think we should travel by foot. It's this way."

"Sure you don't want to fly?" I walked after him, in the direction of the witches' area of town. "I'm joking. I doubt I can carry someone else along for the ride. But it strikes me that patrolling the forest on foot isn't the most efficient method for finding monsters. Did they make you stay there all night?"

"No, I managed to get a few hours' sleep before sunrise," he said. "As for patrolling, you wouldn't be able to see through the trees from above, and it's easier to find footprints on ground level."

"Have you found any? You said you'd update me..."

A moment passed. His shoulders were tense, while the easy smile he'd worn before was gone. "No. Not for lack of trying. I only patrol the witches' area of the forest, since the werewolves and the elves aren't keen to let outsiders in. If the elves find anything, I told them to let me know."

I nearly stopped walking. "You've spoken to them?"

"Yes. Is that so strange?"

"I ran into one on witch territory once," I said. "Can't remember if I told you or not, but I got the impression they're not huge fans of witches. But I guess, since you're not one..."

"They're not fans of humans in general," he said, with a shrug. "But I made a commitment to finding that creature, and they expect me to honour it."

I shivered a little. He was willingly putting himself into harm's way. Sure, I knew it couldn't be the first time he'd done it—far from it—and yet...

"What if it's worse than a shifter, or... wait, how *do* you deal with a rogue werewolf?" I looked sideways at him. "You're not armed."

"Not visibly."

"Oh." *Oh.* Hidden weapons. Of course he wouldn't walk around unarmed, however casual his jeans and jacket looked. My imagination filled in the blanks, and I suppressed the urge to risk a look to see what he might be hiding.

"I don't kill them if I can help it." His tone was slightly hesitant. "I know my old job title implies it, but it's a last resort if anything, and rogues are usually left for the pack to deal with."

Wait. Did he assume I was mad at him? Or scared of him? "It's fine. I'm just..." *worried. A little. Okay. A lot.* He wasn't a pushover, but I knew what those werewolf teeth looked like close up.

"I hope things calm down soon," he said. "I like you a lot, Blair. I don't want this... case, to drive a wedge between us."

My jaw dropped for a moment before I reeled it under control. Nobody would willingly spend this much time on my weird schemes if they didn't like me, but in any other circumstances, I'd have placed him in the category of 'several miles out of my league'. The life I'd left behind in the normal world would never have included dating someone who made every heterosexual female in the vicinity go weak-kneed, but I'd long since left that life behind.

I managed a smile. "I like you, too. And I wish we had the chance for a date. A real one."

"We will," he said. "If not before this is over, then after, for sure. Deal?"

"Deal."

7

Nathan halted outside a wide house set apart from its neighbours. The wizard did well for himself, with or without his vampire ancestor's inheritance. Speaking of vampires, they must have decided to leave him alone, unless they'd already got him to help them access Lord Goddard's house.

I rang the doorbell this time, while Nathan stood at my side. There'd be no reason for the wizard to distrust us, since we didn't have fangs.

"If you're another bloody vampire, I'll turn you into a pincushion," bellowed a voice.

Ah. Maybe not, then.

"We're not vampires," I said.

The door opened a crack. "I've had it with vampires knocking on my door all the time." A grey-haired wizard with a slight paunch opened the door a little more. "You're the new girl."

"I'm Blair. I was at the vampire's house helping

Madame Grey check the wards the other day, so I wondered if it worked for you."

"No," said the wizard. "I drove the vampires away."

"What, you waved garlic at them or…" I broke off at his perplexed expression. Okay, that one must be from normals' interpretations of vampire legends.

"Vampires can't cross water," he explained. "So I created a moat. Elemental spells aren't my strong suit, but it sent them packing." He bared his yellow teeth in a grin.

I looked down. Now he mentioned it, the ground did look damp.

"That seems a bit harsh. They just wanted to know if you could get into your deceased relative's house."

"Even if I could, I have no interest in his inheritance," he said. "He was my great-great-great-great uncle and disowned my entire family over a century ago. Now I'm the only one left."

Wow. "Oh. I'm sorry about that. But… I don't know if the vampires told you, but there's an active police investigation going on, and clues might be inside Lord Goddard's house. Since there are blood wards outside, I guess you're the only person who can enter."

He scratched his chin. "I've spoken to the police, too. Gargoyles. First them and now the undead, and all because my ancestor was idiotic enough to get himself bitten a few centuries ago."

I blinked. "Okay. I get that it's not really your problem, but if you can undo the wards to let the police in, your part in this will be done. There aren't any vampires around at the moment."

"Well," he said, looking over my shoulder at Nathan. "It

does sound do-able when you put it like that. Who's this one? Hunter, right?"

"Former hunter," said Nathan. "I believe the vampires have given up the search for now. Aren't you interested in seeing what your ancestor had to hide? There are rumours of riches hidden inside that house."

"I have everything I need," said the wizard.

"The vampires aren't going to quit," I told him. "If you get in there first, you can squash the rumours before they get out of hand. They're already telling everyone in town that he kept a solid gold coffin in there."

"Goddess, fine," he muttered, looking up at the sky. Since it was summer, it wouldn't get dark until much later. "I have a perfectly serviceable house of my own. I don't need another one. And I want absolutely nothing to do with those bloodsuckers."

True. Not a word he'd said had been a lie.

"Okay," I said. "He probably knew that. But since the other vampires haven't found a will, they have to go by guesswork. If you get in, you'll solve that problem, help the police, and you won't even have to say a word to the vampires."

He nodded slowly. "Fine. But if my delightful ancestor has decided to ward the place, I won't be setting foot in there without protection of my own." His attention moved to Nathan, then me. "It's plain to see my ancestor had enemies, and it wouldn't surprise me if he left more traps inside the house as another precaution."

Unfortunately, he might be right.

"How about we go with you, then?" I said. "Nathan is an ex-hunter, and I'm a witch." More or less, anyway.

"I know who you are," he said. "Yes... you and your partner will do. We'll go now."

Partner. My heart leap-frogged around at the word, but I schooled my face into a composed expression as I looked at Nathan. "You don't have anywhere you have to be, right?"

"No, I have an hour." He checked his watch. "Just about. I can see through most paranormal disguises, so I doubt there'll be anything in there I have no experience in."

Coming from anyone else, I'd have said his tone sounded cocky, but he was too matter-of-fact. Like it was truth. And my truth-sensing ability agreed.

Oh boy.

Once the wizard had detoured back into his house to grab some props, we set off for Lord Goddard's mansion. I hoped the other vampires hadn't got any ideas and decided to come back. While Peter marched ahead, I hung back with Nathan. "Are you sure you know what to expect? Because I'm not really experienced with the sort of defences a paranoid wizard-turned-vampire might leave on his house."

"You did an excellent job of convincing him to help, Blair. Don't sell yourself short."

I flushed to the tips of my ears. "It was that or listen to the vampires complaining for weeks." I was pretty sure Vincent would agree, but Nathan wouldn't appreciate me bringing up the vampire again. I had zero feelings for the vampire—the age gap alone, not to mention the creep factor, was enough to put me off—but Nathan's tone whenever I mentioned him made it clear that he distrusted the elder vampire. He didn't strike me as the jealous type, but I still had trouble believing he was interested in *me,* so I wouldn't kill the mood by bringing up my cat's undead BFF.

"Where are these wards?" asked the wizard, halting in front of the vampire's manor house.

"There." I pointed to the gates. "The vampires got cut pretty badly when they walked in. Even Madame Grey couldn't bring down the wards, since they're tuned into the blood of anyone who belongs to his family. They won't hurt you, for that reason."

"If Madame Grey's sure..." The wizard walked up to the gates. There was a shimmer across the air before him, and Nathan straightened up at my side.

"He's bypassing the ward," he muttered. "It does recognise him."

"How'd you know?" I asked.

"I can see through illusions. There are tricks to it."

That must be handy... wait a moment.

"Glamour, too?" I blurted, against my better judgement. Surely not. I'd been told the glamour hiding my true appearance was so impenetrable that even I couldn't see through it unless I went underneath the Fairy Falls. And it'd snapped back into place when I'd left.

"You mean fairy glamour?" he asked. "Not to the same degree, but it's designed to keep humans out. Witch illusions usually aren't. Why?"

Because I'm *keeping you out, apparently.*

The wizard clicked the gate open before I could think of a response. "It does react to my blood," he remarked. "Come on. Let's see what my dearest ancestor wanted to hide."

"Er... are we allowed to go after you?" I asked. "I

thought—I heard something about invitations being important to vampires. They can't enter one another's homes without permission."

"I shut down the wards," he said. "Switched them off. Can't promise the house might not turn on you anyway, but you should be able to get in."

Nathan walked to the gate, carefully opening it, then went inside. "Coming, Blair?"

"I wouldn't miss it," I responded.

The gate didn't kick either of us out, and we followed the wizard into the extensive grounds. It was a good job the whole place was protected, because a monster of any size could have hidden behind one of the dozens of ornamental trees filling the space within. I held my breath when Peter opened the front door, but no vampire booby trap exploded in our faces. So far, so good.

The inside of the hall was dark and gloomy, as befitting the home of an ancient vampire. Haunted houses were *not* my thing. I'd been on a ghost tour of York on a day trip once and spent the whole time hiding behind Rebecca, my best friend. She'd found the whole thing hilarious. Maybe it was my sensitivity to the paranormal at work. After all, ghosts *were* real. I'd met one just a couple of weeks ago.

I half expected to see a ghostly vampire floating around, but there was nothing but dust, wide rooms with high ceilings and expensive furniture, and—

"Trapdoor!" The wizard raised his wand in time to slam the door shut before something huge and luminous fell on our heads.

"What was that?" I asked.

"I believe it was an inflatable vampire."

I stifled a laugh that was mostly relief, and kept one eye on the ceiling as I followed. I turned on my levitating boots to the lowest setting, so I wouldn't have to watch the floor, too.

We found three more booby traps. Two, the wizard derailed. The third was a bag of flour balanced above the door frame. The wizard caught it in his hand, but not before whiteness drenched all of us like snow. I burst out laughing, the sound echoing back at me, until he waved his wand and the flour vanished.

"Whereabouts would he hide a will?" I asked. "Maybe in a secret safe in the basement. Or attic."

In the basement, we found nothing but dust and more booby traps. The first floor yielded no results, either. It'd take several people to search the whole house, and splitting up wouldn't be a good idea, so we had to go one room at a time.

Peter exclaimed when he opened the door to the master bedroom.

"There it is."

It was apparent that Lord Goddard did sleep in a coffin, but an oak one, not solid gold.

The wizard strode into the room, opened the coffin lid, and then let out a howl. A mousetrap covered his wrist. Swearing under his breath, he prodded it with his wand and it unsnapped.

"You'd think he did know he was going to die," I said. "That, or he had entirely too much time on his hands."

"It's me," said the wizard. "My presence is setting off the traps, same as the wards. They'd go off whether he expected to die or not."

Hmm. I wasn't entirely convinced. "Is it common for

wizards to set up booby traps to activate when they have a break-in?"

"Depends on the wizard. He owned this house when he *was* one, so I guess the traps have been set up for a while. That, or he owned a pet..."

A tittering laugh came from above. My attention snapped onto the ceiling, and a winged creature flitted past. It had pointed ears, a long twig-like body, and delicate, fluttering wings.

Fairy. No—pixie. I'd seen illustrations in a book at the local shop, back when I'd first found out I was half fairy.

"Did you booby-trap the place?" I asked the pixie.

The little creature descended, bowed, and disappeared in a shower of glitter.

The others stared at me. "Who were you talking to?"

"The..." Oh no. The pixie must have glamoured itself, so nobody but another fairy could see it. "I thought I saw, well, a ghost."

Lie.

Stop it. There was no way I was exposing my secret in front of the wizard, at least not until I made sense of what'd happened. There was a pixie living here? Since when did vampires befriend fairies? It seemed a weird coincidence, but fairies had chased each other through my dreams ever since I'd been forced to stay away from the falls when I should have been meeting with my family. Maybe I was cracking up after all.

I didn't miss the concerned look on Nathan's face as he stepped away from the coffin. It contained nothing else, despite the mousetrap. The wizard muttered about ghosts and moved to the wardrobe. He probably thought I *was* cracking up. But I knew what I'd seen.

I kept one eye out for the pixie as we searched every corner of the room and then moved onto the next. Despite searching each and every hiding place, we still found no signs of a will or inheritance, nor any clues that might point to the killer.

"I have to leave if I want to make it to my post on time," Nathan said. "I think it's wise for you to go home before dark, too, Blair. We've searched every room."

But where did the pixie go?

"I'll leave the wards off," said the wizard. "Those meddling vampires can wander in and out to their heart's content. There's nothing here. And I'll tell the police that, too."

"We can detour there on the way back," Nathan said. "So you don't have to deal with Steve later."

He grunted. "He'll probably take me to task for entering the house without him there."

"Maybe we'll tell him we saw a ghost," I said. "That'd put him off."

The wizard fixed his beady eyes on me. "I thought you said you did see one."

"I probably imagined it," I said. "I'm not a fan of haunted houses. I guess we'd know if his ghost had stuck around, right? Is that common?"

"No, especially with vampires," said the wizard. "They live such long lives, I imagine a trip to the afterlife is a relief."

I just wished I knew what Lord Goddard had been thinking with this setup. Did he want to keep intruders out, or had he hidden his will elsewhere? And where in the world had that pixie gone?

Steve the Gargoyle accosted us in the entryway to the police station. "Why am I not surprised it's you, Wilkes?"

"I persuaded Peter to undo the wards on Lord Goddard's house," I said to him. "That way, anyone can go in and out of the house. In fact, you can go there right now."

I decided not to mention that we hadn't necessarily tripped *every* booby trap.

"Is that so?" he said. "Maybe I will."

"Not after dark," added the hard-faced female gargoyle at the reception desk.

He scowled at her. "I'll thank you not to patronise me. No monster would dare attack me, let alone a ghost."

We took that as our cue to leave. At least the police knew the wizard had been to the house, even if they seemed little inclined to actually do anything useful.

"Will you be okay walking home alone?" Nathan asked, glancing over his shoulder as we left the station. "We can reschedule our date for Friday. I'll ask not to be put on any shifts that evening."

"Sure. That sounds great."

The wizard exited the police station behind me, and Nathan waved goodbye, heading in the opposite direction. Peter grunted. "Useless, the lot of them."

"The gargoyles?" I asked. "Yeah. They are. Hope Steve goes in there tonight and gets haunted."

"That was no ghost," growled the wizard. "And you, Blair Wilkes, really need to be careful. I want nothing more to do with this investigation, ever again."

He walked off before I could respond. Maybe the

house had creeped him out more than I'd thought. He hadn't seen the pixie, right?

I think I'm done with vampires for the foreseeable future. Veronica was right. They were really too much bother.

When I got home, it was to find Alissa perched on the sofa with her feet up, reading a 'Wicked Witchery' magazine, a box of cookies from the local bakery open on the coffee table.

"Where in the world have you been all day?" she asked, in a slightly croaky voice. She'd been worse off than me last night, while today's adventures had made me entirely forget my hangover.

Where to start? "One of the vampires suspected of killing Lord Goddard insisted on telling me in person that he didn't do it. Blame that one on Vincent. Then we detoured to speak to the wizard—"

"Who's 'we'?"

"Nathan," I said. "He's the one the vampire contacted. I guess because the police sent him. The wizard, Peter, has had vampires coming after him all week wanting access to Lord Goddard's old house. I persuaded him to take down the wards and we had a look around."

I took a seat next to her on the sofa, and told her about our misadventures in the elder vampire's manor.

Her eyes widened. "That's... wow. Did you tell Nathan what you saw?"

"No. I wasn't going to say a word to Nathan with Peter —the wizard—there, but he said something weird to me after we left the police station. I think he might have known. I also think Lord Anderson did, too. I... he was trying to read my mind and I shut him out. I don't even know how I did it."

"Shut him out?" she echoed. "How?"

I shook my head, taking a cookie from the open box on the coffee table. "Haven't a clue. It's like… I knew he was trying to read my thoughts, and I somehow stopped him. Anyway, he seemed to want me to use my ability to prove he wasn't guilty, but the police weren't there so it was kind of pointless. Blame Vincent for telling him that I was the best person to talk to. Sky was probably involved, too. Where is he, anyway?"

"Went out hunting."

"Or socialising with vampires." I took a bite of the cookie, reminded that I hadn't eaten a proper meal all day. "Most cats hunt rodents, not the living dead. They also don't drag their owners into murder investigations."

"Sounds like you walked into part of it on purpose."

I smiled. "The old house was intriguing. Who wouldn't want to know what was inside it? Even Madame Grey couldn't bring those wards down."

"Maybe that was the fairy's doing, too."

My smile slipped away. "I want to talk to it. If pixies can talk, which I don't think they can. But I'm sure it knew what I was."

And so, apparently, did everyone else. Except Nathan.

Right. I'll tell him on our next date. This was getting ridiculous. It wasn't like I'd committed a crime or been one of the paranormals he'd locked up. All I'd done was lack information on my family—which wasn't my fault. He'd probably be a little annoyed to say the least that I'd kept it from him for this long, especially if he cared about me as much as he said he did.

My heart flipped over. There was one upside to the

lie-sensing ability... every word he'd said was a hundred percent sincere.

"What're you grinning about? Please say you and Nathan at least had time to schedule another date."

"We did," I said. "Provided no more vampires, murders, or monsters get in the way this time."

As long as my adventurous cat was around, that might be expecting too much.

8

I dedicated Sunday to practising magic, determined to beat the odds and learn to cast a spell with a wand, whenever I wanted. I might be barred from practical lessons, but Rita hadn't said I couldn't practise outside of the classroom.

Alissa cast a shielding spell on the flat to avoid accidentally damaging Madame Grey's property, while Sky perched on top of a cabinet to watch from afar.

"Turn purple," I yelled at the cup I was practising on, waving my wand aggressively. "Left, flick—"

Purple paint exploded from the end. As the shielding spell covered the whole flat, the splatters of paint hung in mid-air like glitter-free tinsel.

Alissa burst out laughing. "I think you just invented a new one."

"Really?"

"Nah, you aimed too far left. Try not to wave your wand like a tennis racket, too."

"I think magic must be designed for people with good

hand-eye coordination,' I said. "I hardly know my left hand from my right one."

"Wait." Alissa waved her own wand and made the purple paint vanish. "Maybe that's it. I know you're right-handed, but it's… it's not impossible for your wand to be different."

I frowned at her. "What… try my left hand?"

I'd never thought about it. But when I'd accidentally used magic without a wand… the spell hadn't come from my right hand.

"It's worth a try," Alissa said.

Maybe. Come to think of it, when I'd been lying there in Mr Falconer's shop and I'd grabbed the nearest wand, I'd used my left hand. But I was generally right-handed, and couldn't even write a coherent word with my left one. At this point, though, I was willing to try anything.

I switched the wand to my other hand, and immediately, a rush of heat enveloped my fingertips. I pointed my wand at the second mug on the table, waved it, and the mug turned purple.

"Yes!" I did a victory dance that made Sky look at me like he was seriously considering adopting another witch. I didn't care a bit. I'd finally done magic!

———

After work on Monday, I made my way to my magic lesson in high spirits, only to find another note from Rita saying she was in a meeting with Madame Grey. I sat down in my usual seat in the front row, deciding to get on with some theory work until the meeting was over. I wasn't about to wait another day to explain my epiphany about my magic. It hadn't been an accident this time.

After a few minutes, a commotion of slamming doors and shouts came from the lobby. I looked up from my notes at the sound of a wolf's howl. *Not the vampires again?*

I jumped to my feet, anticipating another bleeding vampire. Instead, three werewolves stood in the lobby—easily recognisable, because they were all huge and blond and related to Callie.

"Where is Madame Grey?" bellowed the one I recognised as her cousin. The other two were her brother, and her father, leader of the pack. Oh no.

The moment they turned on me, images of snapping teeth and shifting forms into giant furry bodies assailed my vision. Chief Donovan was the biggest of the three of them, but they were all huge and muscular, formidable even when they weren't in their shifted forms.

"She's in a coven meeting," I said, shrinking beneath the pack chief's gaze.

Rita opened the meeting room door and peered out at them. "You might have the decency to knock first."

"How dare you speak of decency?" said Callie's brother in a raspy voice. "Our fellow shifter was murdered."

My stomach turned over. *Oh, no.*

"This is the vampires' doing," added Callie's cousin.

Chief Donovan marched to the half-open door of the coven meeting. "This is Chief Donovan of the Northwest Pack," he said, his voice clear and loud. "I wish to speak with Madame Grey."

The woman herself marched to Rita's side, her wand glowing with silver light. "Is there a reason you interrupted our meeting?"

"There's been a murder," growled Chief Donovan. "One of our own was found dead on the border of your territory."

"In the woods?" she asked. "Might I ask how he died?"

Chief Donovan let out a low growl that made the small hairs on my arms stand up. "Not a shifter killing. His wounds aren't visible to our eyes, yet he's dead."

If they couldn't see the wounds… a vampire's bite might easily be responsible. But jumping to that conclusion would set the tensions between the two groups off like a cauldron of fireworks.

"Whereabouts is he?" she asked. "If you want my help, I'll need to see the body."

"He's with the pack," he growled. "There will be blood for this."

"The council cannot take steps until it's confirmed that he was murdered," said Madame Grey patiently. "We certainly won't allow unfounded accusations to spread without proof. It's vital to the safety and security of this town that you keep your tempers under control rather than accusing your fellow paranormals."

"Safety and security?" growled Callie's cousin. "One of our own was murdered."

No kidding. Had the werewolf fallen victim to the same killer who'd gone after the vampires, or had the vampires blamed the pack and retaliated?

Madame Grey stepped past the werewolves into the lobby, letting the meeting room door swing closed behind her. "Allow me to converse with the Chief in private," she told the other two werewolves. "We will see to it that this is put under investigation, but you'll need to cooperate with the rest of the council. Have you reported the murder to the police?"

"The police are inept," said Chief Donovan. "They are also cowardly."

Unfortunately, he wasn't wrong.

"Ask the police chief to file a report," Madame Grey ordered. "Otherwise, there's no basis to investigate the death as a murder.

"There's no need," said Callie's cousin. "We know who did it. The vampires blame us for murdering their own and have paid us back in kind. There will be bloodshed."

"How did he die?" I blurted. "Because if there aren't any wounds, it probably isn't a vampire." For all our sakes, I really hoped it wasn't.

"What business is it of yours?" growled the chief.

"It affects all of us if you declare war on one another," I said, which was technically true. Too many of my friends were tangled up in this. Nathan and Alissa—not to mention my cat.

He stepped close to me. "That's right, you and your hunter friend."

"He has nothing to do with this," I interjected. "I'm not involved. I have no arguments with anyone."

"And the fact that you've been seen fraternising with the vampires on more than one occasion is nothing?" Callie's cousin asked softly.

"What is this, school?" I rolled my eyes, pretending his loud voice and intimidating stature didn't bother me at all —to say nothing of the wolf beneath the surface. "I'm not getting involved in your cliques. If every one of you hadn't been outright rude to me except for Callie, maybe I wouldn't mind socialising with you and not the vampires."

If hell freezes over, I thought, but didn't say that last part aloud.

Madame Grey cleared her throat loudly. "I would advise you to be careful in the forest at this late hour," she said. "Let the police take control of the investigation, and ask me if you have any other concerns. I'm not about to step into the middle of your feud with the vampires, but remember how long our peace has lasted, and why. Go, now."

The werewolves sloped off, muttering angrily. Madame Grey swept back into the meeting room, too, without so much as a glance at me.

Rita turned to me. "Blair, I would go home. I don't expect you to concentrate on wand-work today."

"But I need to talk to—"

And she was gone. Leaving me and my left-handed wand behind.

Great. I wouldn't push Madame Grey right now, and considering there was a killer out there, wandering around alone at night wasn't the smartest idea. Even for Nathan. I hoped he'd been warned not to go anywhere near werewolf territory tonight.

In my dream, I was flying... flying...

The flat door crashed open, and I jolted awake. "Sky?"

No response came from the cat, but footsteps sounded in the living room. I checked the time—two in the morning—and opened my bedroom door to find Alissa standing in the living room, looking utterly lost.

"Sorry I woke you, Blair." She looked a mess, hair

dishevelled, clothes wrinkled, yet her tone was surprisingly sober. "I've had a night of it."

"You weren't hauled in by the police again?" She hadn't been in when I came back, because she was working, so I'd assumed she was safe. I'd texted her with news of the murder, but received no response before I'd fallen into an exhausted slumber.

"No," she said. "Bryan found the body."

"Oh," I said.

"Exactly." She grimaced, flopping on the sofa. Roald rubbed himself against her face, obviously picking up on her distress. She lifted her head. "The werewolves think the vampires retaliated against them. You know... vampire bites are lethal to werewolves. They haven't done a full autopsy yet, so all they're doing is yelling accusations. But Bryan called me with a warning that since he found the body, the police have him listed as a suspect."

"What, for murdering another werewolf?" I hadn't known vampire bites were lethal to werewolves, either.

"The police don't think it's part of their feud," said Alissa. "I've heard a dozen theories, but the most common one is that it's some independent killer targeting paranormals in general, not one particular group."

I thought this over. It made sense, but the feud was a more obvious explanation. "What, like the monster in the woods? But the wolves said that there were no obvious signs of the cause of death."

"When Steve has a target, he goes all-out, and unfortunately, he's convinced that one of the vampires is attempting to stoke tensions between the werewolves and their fellow vamps. He's likely to drag Keith in for questioning tomorrow, on top of Bryan, who's under suspicion from both sides. It's his own fault, though. If he hadn't taken it upon himself to come to the hospital that day in the first place, he'd be in the clear."

"It seems weird that he did that to begin with," I said. "Unless it's not the first time he's tried to win you back?"

Alissa's mouth twisted. "What you saw at the New Moon? Picture that, every night for the first two weeks after our breakup. All his tragic love songs are based on our relationship."

"That's creepy. Really creepy."

"It's not like he crossed any visible lines," she said. "The hospital is open to the public. But he's only visited me at work twice, and the first time, I nearly gave him a reason to make it a permanent stay. Let's just say it involved needles."

I laughed, despite myself. "You should have done that this time."

"I would have done if he'd reached me before the nurses threw him out. They know what he's like. Honestly, I wouldn't shed a tear if he gets locked up, but he's no murderer."

Hmm. "Let them figure out the cause of death first. Then…" Then what? Did we have a vampire-werewolf feud playing out, or something more? There was no way to get an unbiased answer from either the vamps *or* the werewolves. And it wasn't fair for the newbie vampire to keep getting dragged into it either—though the question remained of whichever vampire had been the one to bite him. I'd forgotten all about that, in the wake of everything else that'd happened.

Alissa got to her feet. "I'm going to bed. Maybe I'll

think of a plan in the morning. Don't you have to be up for work?"

"Yep." I yawned. "I didn't even get to explain my wand situation to Rita, so I'm still off the list for classes. I can do some poking around after work."

"No more poking around," she said, making for her bedroom door. "I don't know *what* to think, but I'm inclined to agree with the police. This person is after paranormals in general, and it might not be a coincidence that he picked the two most volatile groups in town."

"Three, if you count the elves."

But the only link between the two cases was that the bodies had been found in the woods. What kind of killer set a monster on some of his victims and poisoned others?

I returned to my room, finding Sky sprawled on my pillow. "How did you get in?"

"Miaow."

I stroked him. His fur was ice-cold. "What were you doing, hanging around with vampires again?"

The cat dug his claws into my bed, forcing me to squash onto the bed next to him. It was like trying to sleep beside a fluffy ice block. "I don't suppose you know who our killer is?"

"Miaow."

"Thought not." My eyelids fluttered closed.

———

I woke with a resounding thud as I hit the floor on my side. Groaning, I crawled upright and saw Sky sitting on the windowsill, his fur on end.

I gasped. The little pixie from the vampire's house was outside my window.

"Wait!"

I grabbed my slippers and ran from the flat, barely remembering to snatch up my keys on the way out. I wore only thin cotton pyjamas, but I hardly cared. My feet skidded in the hallway as I sprinted to the back door.

But he'd gone. There was no sign of the pixie, just the merest sprinkling of fairy dust on the lawn.

9

Shockingly, my focus levels at work that day were at an all-time low.

"You look like a pixie just crapped in your coffee," said Bethan from behind a stack of papers.

I nearly *dropped* my coffee. *It's just a figure of speech.* "Yeah, right. Rough night."

"I heard," said Bethan. "That's the only reason I'm not taking you to task on the boss's behalf for calling the last three clients the wrong names."

I winced. "Sorry. Alissa came back in the early hours of the morning panicking about the werewolf's murder. She's worried about getting arrested again. Since her ex found the body."

"Ugh, that guy," said Bethan. "I remember him. He wasn't on the suspect list for the vampire, was he?"

"Only because he got caught trying to sneak into the hospital to give her flowers right before the vampire died. Do you think he might have done it?"

"No clue," she said. "I don't like him. I also can't say I'm much of a fan of the elder vampires, either."

"As opposed to the younger ones?" I asked. "Your mother said the same. Aren't all vampires more or less the same, give or take a few centuries?"

"Not the ones who didn't use to play by the rules," Lizzie said from across the desk, her chin in her hand. "Laws change with the times, and the vampires were never happy when they brought in the stringent new laws against biting normals. Most of us who were born in the last twenty or thirty years didn't know that it used to be legal, but the older residents do. They remember."

"Oh," I said. "What, did it used to be legal to bite people whenever they wanted to?"

"Normals," said Bethan. "Yeah. It's bad. Our history isn't that pleasant. There were paranormals who wanted power and were happy to abuse it. And then there were some elder vamps who thought vampires were superior to humans, and for that reason, they should be allowed to use that power to take whatever they wanted. The hunters were part of the force against that... which is why the elder vampires don't get on with the hunters."

I remembered Lord Anderson's reaction to Nathan. Now him wanting to talk to me instead made slightly more sense. Didn't exactly explain why the wolves hated him, but I guessed that his own actions in bringing rogues to justice probably spoke for themselves.

"Right," I said. "So... might it be an elder vampire behind this? I guess it depends how the werewolf died. They didn't mention finding bite marks."

"I wouldn't have thought so," said Bethan. "It was humans they felt superior to, not other paranormals. Wild werewolves were even worse than the vampires were when it came to attacking humans… and I'm going to stop talking before Callie overhears."

"Wise idea," said Lizzie.

I turned the new information over in my head as I forced myself to read over the client list more carefully this time. An elder vampire had died. Had that been deliberate? What was the connecting factor between the two deaths?

I jumped when the boss appeared behind me. "Callie has gone home to her family," she announced. "I'll need one of you to watch the desk in her place."

"I'll do it," I said. *I think the clients would probably agree.*

Also, if I admitted it, I kind of hoped Nathan would walk in so we could have a proper conversation.

Ten minutes into watching the door, I wished I'd stayed in the office instead. We rarely had visitors unless someone was running interviews, and I had too much pent-up energy to have any patience for sitting inert at a desk. I opened the desk drawer and found a device shaped like a spinning top and picked it up—and jumped when it grew wings and flitted around my head like a tiny hummingbird. I lunged to catch it and missed, nearly knocking the desk over.

Of course, that's when the door opened and Nathan walked in.

Before my brain quite caught up with my actions, my wand was in my hand—my left hand—and I'd executed a perfect summoning spell. Nathan's eyes widened as the bird-thing shot over his head, back into my hand.

I gaped at it. *Whoa.*

"Blair?" he said. "Is that—?"

"I have no idea what it is." I put the bird-thing down on the desk. "It's Callie's. I'm on desk duty today."

His gaze dropped to my hand and a frown marred his face. Of course, he was too observant not to notice my surprise display of witchcraft wasn't quite right.

"Ah, Nathan," said Veronica, sweeping over to him before I could offer an explanation. "As you may have heard, my receptionist has been inconveniently detained in a murder investigation again. I have Blair watching the desk, and I'd like you to keep an eye on things outside in case anyone else decides to make trouble."

It looked like Veronica's paranoia was back in full force. She returned to her office, and I set the humming-bird-thing back on the desk.

"Are you going to the police station later?" I asked Nathan.

"When they need me. Why?"

"Alissa." I explained our encounter early this morning. "She's worried Keith will end up accused again."

"You're going to get yourself into trouble if you keep worrying about other people more than yourself," he said, but not in a reprimanding tone. "You don't have to feel responsible for their decisions."

A lump grew in my throat. "I guess… in my life before this, people didn't need me to worry about them. They had everything already figured out. Also, my cat is equally concerned, and I have absolutely no control over anything *he* does. I'd just like to know… did they ever work out the cause of the werewolf's death?"

"They did," Nathan said. "Poison."

"The same poison that killed the vampire?"

I already knew the answer.

Steve the Gargoyle was about as pleased to see me as I was to see him.

"You interfering little busybody," he said, crowding the doorway to the police station. "Get out."

"She's with me," Nathan interjected.

"Not good enough. You're in the employ of the council. She's a... nobody."

"That's lovely," I said. "Is Alissa here?"

"Your little witch friend is lucky she's not in our cells with her vampire friend."

"You can't just lock people up on a whim!" I said. "You actually locked Keith in jail? Why?"

"Because he's a major suspect," he growled. "And for your information, I *can* lock people up on a whim."

"You're being absurd," I said. "Keith was under watch when Lord Goddard was killed. And he can't have killed the werewolf. He's new to being a vampire and isn't even part of their group."

It looked like the murders of two powerful paranormals in a short space of time had sent Steve over the edge. "Unfortunately for you, I'm the one in charge," he said, slowly and clearly. "Get out."

Nathan walked me to the door like he was afraid Steve would pounce on me and arrest me the second he turned his back—which was starting to look worryingly likely.

"Alissa's going to be mad," I said. "Lord Goddard's house... did the other vampires get in?"

"No idea," Nathan said. "Why?"

"Well, we haven't cleared up if the first murder was to do with his inheritance or not. I mean, if it's the same killer, then I guess not. Who was the murdered werewolf?"

"You won't get near them, Blair," said Nathan. "They're fiercely protective of their own, and it took long enough for them to get the police to look at the body. In the end, they only cooperated because Steve is an ally of theirs."

Ugh. He would be. Despite having no respect for him, I'd bet Chief Donovan had figured that he needed the police on his side. Since the gargoyles feared the vampires, siding with the werewolves was a natural choice. But it wasn't fair of him to lock Keith up without a trial, and Alissa couldn't intervene without putting her neck on the line again.

But… there might be *one* person who could help us.

"Do you think the vampires will react as badly as the werewolves when they find out someone targeted both of them in the same way?" I asked Nathan.

"Not unless the werewolves directly strike," he said. "The elders don't want war, but they respond to any threat immediately and with violence. It's why they're one of the more unpredictable paranormal types."

"What about fairies?"

I didn't know where the question came from, except that now the words were out there, hanging in the air between us. Horrified at myself, I hoped, stupidly, that the wind had caught my words at that precise moment and he hadn't heard.

He arched a brow. "Fairies? They don't have a council representative. Including the elves. We have yet to hear their opinion on the murder, but they haven't declared war on anyone."

Oh. He must think that I'd meant the killer monster in the woods. "Are you going to the forest now?"

He inclined his head. "Yes. I'll be patrolling again this evening. I'll see you later, Blair."

He returned to the police station, while I mentally berated myself for not taking the opening and telling him what I was. But helping Keith, and Alissa by extension, was more important than chasing pixies.

Leaving the police station, I didn't head home, but up the road past Lord Goddard's mansion. It seemed the vampires had given up on trying to break in, because there was nobody around. One look at the newly reinstated wards told me they wouldn't be getting back inside. So Peter had reset them after all, or they'd switched back on. The vampires wouldn't be pleased, though they were probably a little preoccupied defending themselves from the werewolves' accusations. Hopefully, word wouldn't have reached Vincent yet.

I didn't know if he'd be as easily pushed into action as the others, but Steve feared him, and that was reason enough to ask for his help. As a new vampire, Keith had no reputation to use as a defence. He needed another vampire's help, and while Vincent was out for his own self-interest, surely he wouldn't want an innocent newbie vampire to languish in jail while Steve threw his weight around.

Keith aside, the town's safety was at stake, not to mention the peace that had lasted for centuries here. *Hmm.* Probably best not to use an expression involving the word 'stake' when I made my case to him.

I walked past the mansion and continued uphill. I'd never been to this part of town before, but I'd been told the cemetery was the place where the vampires' council met. Unless Vincent happened to be in one of his usual haunts—and given the level of paranoia surrounding the vampires lately, it didn't look likely—then he'd be there.

The houses on this side of town were larger, grander, and more spread out than those in the witches' territory. It wasn't hard to spot which one belonged to the council, because it was the only house that wasn't surrounded by several layers of warded fences, and stood alone next to the cemetery gates. They presumably didn't keep anything valuable in there. Not that the sooty black bricks and windows curtained in dark shades looked particularly inviting either way, but when I reached the door and knocked, no wards exploded in my face.

I kept my wand close at hand, just in case. *I hope the vampires don't blame me for this situation, too.*

The door opened, and Vincent appeared, his brows rising. "Blair Wilkes. Come to collect your cat?"

"Sky's here? I mean—no, I came to speak to you. I assumed you wouldn't be in the hospital, with things the way they are."

"You thought correctly."

A black furry body pushed between us, wrapping around the vampire's legs. "I knew it," I said to Sky. "Is that where you were last night?"

"He likes to keep me company," said Vincent.

"Do vampires sleep?" I couldn't help asking. "I mean, the stories say you sleep during the day, but they also say you burst into flames in sunlight and can't see your reflection in mirrors."

"All human myths," he said. "Some intentionally cultivated by us. We are, however, generally creatures of the night."

"Really?" I hadn't even considered that aspect, since I'd only run into vampires during daylight hours. "You mean to say you wander around outside at night?"

"Yes. Why?"

I shook my head. "With monsters on the loose in the woods, and a murderer?"

"You forget that my kind are generally considered predators." He said this with a distinct flash of teeth. "We do not, however, trespass on the territory of others. And the forest holds no interest for us."

"Keith got bitten in the forest."

Something flashed in his eyes. "Yes, he did. We have yet to find the perpetrator."

"And... the killer. Did you hear the latest?"

"The werewolf was killed by the same poison that killed Lord Goddard? Yes."

If he hadn't already, he'd have read it from my thoughts. How easily I forgot. And yet—I'd blocked Lord Anderson.

"The werewolf was not killed by one of mine," he said, giving no indication if he'd picked up on my last thought or not. I wished I knew *how* I'd done it, but I needed to play nice with Vincent if I wanted him to help me and Alissa out.

"But the police think it was Keith, which is clearly nonsense," I said to him. "Aren't you going to talk to the police on his behalf? If his wizard family haven't?" I assumed they hadn't, after he'd been forced to leave them to join the vampires.

His expression turned to cold indifference. "We are

not the wolves. We're not a family unit. We have allies, and friendships, and enemies, but the boy will have to remain in custody until his innocence is determined."

I took a step backwards. "Seriously? My best friend is being targeted by association. Is there nothing you can do?"

"If your friend does nothing foolish, she's unlikely to end up in the same position as Keith. If anything, it may serve as a reminder."

I glanced down at Sky in a plea for help. Instead, the cat circled his legs, not making any effort to move over to me. *Traitor.*

"I have no intention of being your enemy, Blair Wilkes," said Vincent. "I do not know who the killer is. Nor do I know the nature of the beast that hides in the woods, but suffice to say, I have no intention of warring with the werewolves over this. They would do well to remember the peace that's existed in this town for so long."

"The witches said the same," I said. "Didn't really get the impression the werewolves cared. They want immediate results, and all we have is endless questions. Why poison?"

"A simple, quick, clean death," he said dispassionately. "Immediate, giving no warning. Their mistake was picking a public place for the first murder, unless they wished to draw attention."

"What else should they have done?" I queried. "It might have escaped your attention, but your fellow vampires are a tiny bit paranoid about security."

"We have reason to be."

"You don't think Lord Goddard and his wards have anything to do with why he was murdered, do you?"

His still expression didn't budge an inch. "You went into his house."

"You didn't know." I frowned. "Really?"

"I can't read all of your thoughts at once," he answered.

His response came a little too quickly. Wait—had I been I blocking his thoughts, too?

"You can read my cat's thoughts," I said. "Right? You can speak to one another."

"I can," he confirmed. "In a way."

"I knew it," I said. "You telepathically contacted him when Alissa was arrested, didn't you?"

"He's a remarkably intelligent animal," he said.

"Where did you two even meet? It's not like I've owned him that long…" Wait a moment. When Sky had first spotted me, I'd been walking past the bookshop… the same bookshop that Vincent himself frequented. "You knew him before. He was at the bookshop when he found me."

Vincent inclined his head. Well, that explained a lot. If Vincent and the cat had known one another for a while, perhaps in time, I'd be able to develop the same connection with him. Stranger things had happened.

"Can you really not tell me anything else about the murder?"

"I know nothing more than what I have told you, Blair," he said. "Now if you'll excuse me, I have a vampire summit to plan."

No lies. He really didn't know who the killer was, and he had no intention of helping Alissa or Keith.

I beckoned to Sky. "All right. We're going home."

10

I walked quickly back to the house, guilt trailing my every step. I'd utterly failed at convincing the elder vampire to intervene. It'd been a long shot anyway. That's what I got for making assumptions.

Sky darted ahead of me, emitting a high-pitched yowl, and skidded to a halt in front of the house.

A large number of flowers were on the doorstep—huge, purple blooms. "What the...?" I looked around in the hope that an explanation would present itself.

"One of you got an admirer?" asked Flora, the witch who lived in the flat above ours. Alissa and I had never really spoken to her before, but she seemed friendly enough. Blond and perky, she ran the local witches' gymnasium.

"Bryan," I said. "Alissa's all-too-persistent ex. Where is Alissa?"

"She went out."

There was only one place she could be—the jail. I'd thought she was the rational one, but maybe neither of us were. If I hadn't gone after the vampire, I might have been able to stop her from doing something reckless.

Once again, I hurried towards the police station. Discordant shouts of rage echoed down the road through the partly open door, while two gargoyles stood outside the jail, squashing any notion I had of sneaking a look inside. The police station was packed out with people. From the loudness of their voices, I'd guess werewolves. *What was Alissa thinking?*

I pushed the door open, inching my way in behind the nearest group of werewolves. Half the pack filled the room, which, on top of the huge muscled gargoyles, meant there was little space left to breathe. It didn't help that the werewolves' high-volume complaints were like standing next to a loudspeaker. I stood on tip-toe, and spotted Alissa pushed to the crowd's edge. I waved at her frantically.

Alissa caught my eye and began elbowing her way through the crowd. The werewolves paid her no more attention than if she was a mouse running under their feet. All their attention was on the gargoyles, and from the words I picked out amongst the general yelling, they were immensely displeased with the police taking over the investigation into the death of one of their own pack members.

"Alissa!" I beckoned her to follow me out the door. "C'mon. You shouldn't be hanging about here while they're throwing a collective tantrum."

"It's the body," she said, ducking outside behind me. "They did a more thorough investigation of... of the werewolf's body. They found bite marks. *Vampire* bite marks."

"What? I thought the wolf was poisoned."

"They're—" She glanced over her shoulder, her expression distraught. "They're trying to persuade Steve to join their cause and round up every vampire until they find the killer."

"So they don't believe it was Keith?"

"Alone? No. They think it's a conspiracy on behalf of the vampires as a collective."

I swore. "That's absurd. I just spoke to Vincent and he doesn't know who did it. We should go."

"And he wasn't lying?" she asked.

"Of course not. He's not interested in declaring war. I'm getting the impression this feud is mostly one-sided."

"Did a vampire tell you that?" She glanced over her shoulder at the jail, but no werewolves followed us.

"Nathan did." I began to walk back down the road, and to my relief, she followed me. "He's dealt with both. I guess the werewolves are more hot-tempered, so that's why."

"The vampires are subtler than that," she said. "But they won't be when it comes down to blows."

"Exactly," I said. "I get that the werewolves would jump to that conclusion from the bite marks, but Keith himself got bitten by someone acting as a rogue. What if it was the same one?"

"Right." Her lips pursed. "It'd make sense, considering both were in the woods. What *doesn't* make sense is that both victims were killed by poisoning. Keith wasn't poisoned."

I frowned. "Good point. That's downright weird. Unless we have three different villains running around.

One of them eating people, one of them snacking on them, and another using poison."

"Weirder things have happened, but Keith isn't responsible," she said firmly. "I told Steve that. I don't know what more I can do."

"Persuade Vincent to step in to defend him?"

"If you couldn't convince him, I doubt I could," she said.

"He's not that much of a fan of me." I dug my hands in my pockets. "He prefers my cat. Unless I blocked him from reading my thoughts, too, but he wouldn't admit it if I did."

"I forgot you said you could do that," Alissa said. "Which… wow. I can't blame him for being a little ticked off. I don't know anyone else who can shut out a vampire."

"Just another weird Blair thing. Like having a left-handed wand. I need to tell Madame Grey about that, too, but it's looking like she's going to have to intervene in a potential war at any moment now. Do none of the werewolves want a peaceful solution?"

"Not if the gargoyles rise to their bait," she said. "The more reasonable ones are getting utterly shouted down. I'm going to call my grandmother and see if she's available, because at this point, it *is* her business."

We turned into the road leading to our house. "Oh, I should mention," I said. "I found flowers on our doorstep. I'm guessing someone left them for you." Nathan would have left a note, and I hadn't seen one.

She swore under her breath. "Why? Does he really have to?"

The house came into view. The flowers had gone… but

a body lay beside the doorstep, the flowers clutched in her hands.

Flora, our neighbour.

I gasped. "Oh no."

Alissa picked up speed, and I ran alongside her, halting breathlessly at the doorstep. "Please say she isn't dead."

Alissa dropped to her knees alongside her and felt for a pulse. "She's alive."

I'd never been so grateful to be best friends with a magical healer. "How—?"

"I think it was a spell," whispered Alissa. "The flowers."

The huge purple petals had spread over Flora's body, where she'd dropped them. "A booby trap?"

"Looks that way." Alissa pulled out her wand and flicked the flowers' remains off Flora's body. Then she muttered a few words, her wand weaving patterns above Flora's face.

Flora slowly sat up, a dazed expression on her face. "What...?"

"Don't move too fast," Alissa said quickly. "I think you were attacked. Did you pick up the flowers?"

She nodded, her eyes wide, frightened. "Yes. There was a spell... I think it knocked me out."

"I know of that spell," Alissa said, in her calm nurse's voice. "It won't cause you long-term damage. Just take it easy for a while, okay?"

The flowers hadn't been meant for Flora—but did they mean Bryan had tried to attack one of us?

Flora dipped her head. "I will. I'm going to go and lie down for a bit."

"Let me know if you need anything," Alissa called after

her. She looked down at the flowers, biting her lip. "Were they just there on the doorstep?"

I nodded. "I planned to pick them up, but when I heard you were at the jail, I panicked and left her to take care of them. If I'd touched them…"

"I think it's a safe bet one of us was the target," she said, her hands fisting at her sides. "The house is warded, and so is our flat. The person who left them there didn't get inside, at least. We need to report this."

"What—back to the police station again? Why not call them?"

"They never answer the phone," she said. "Doubt they can hear it over all those werewolves, besides."

"Precisely what I was thinking. Maybe we should bring Madame Grey, so they clear off? I don't want the whole world to know we're on the killer's hit list."

My blood chilled. A close call—yet the attack hadn't been fatal. And how in the world were we supposed to get past the howling werewolves and the griping gargoyles to ask for help?

As we'd both expected, the way into the police station was still blocked by werewolves. I doubted Steve would ever have let anyone else in town hang around making a nuisance of themselves for longer than five minutes. Even my interrogation hadn't lasted that long.

Alissa and I managed to squeeze through the doors and past grumbling werewolves to the reception desk, where the stocky female gargoyle receptionist was crammed into a narrow office chair.

"You again?" she said. "Didn't I already tell you to leave?"

"We need to report an attack," I said, but werewolf yowls swallowed my voice.

I spotted Steve in the doorway to the room where they'd had the first body. I guessed every werewolf remotely related to the victim had shown up to check the reports were true. And probably to accuse every vampire who'd ever annoyed them.

"Excuse me?" Alissa shouted to him, with Madame Grey-style steeliness. "I'm here to report an attempt on my life."

Steve cocked his head. "You're what?"

"Someone just left an illegal magical trap on my doorstep," Alissa said, in the same loud, clear voice. "I'd like to file a report."

"Get in line," he growled.

"You've been talking to the same people for hours," she said. "According to the laws of the council, on Madame Grey's orders, you're not supposed to show bias to one group over another."

Several of the werewolves dropped their voices, muttering amongst themselves.

Steve shoved his way towards us. "Talk to Clare, my receptionist. And get out."

I'd never seen Alissa come close to losing her temper before, but I wouldn't have been surprised to see smoke pouring out of her ears. She stormed back to the recep-tion desk. "This is ridiculous. He locked up Keith with no evidence but can't spare five minutes to listen to me?"

The female gargoyle got to her feet, nearly tipping the desk onto us. "Tell me. Or tell nobody."

Alissa said through gritted teeth, "Someone sent a

booby-trapped spell to our flat disguised as a bouquet of flowers. It nearly killed our neighbour."

"Obviously, it's your vampire friend," she said.

"He can't send explosives from jail, even if he's responsible," she pointed out. "Which he isn't."

"He had an accomplice."

We might as well have had an argument with the wall. It'd have been a million times more fulfilling, too.

"He's not the killer," I said. "Or maybe he is, but he can't be the one who sent the flowers. That happened after he'd already been locked in jail."

"And I'll call in Madame Grey," Alissa added. "Council meeting or not, if someone targets one of her granddaughters, heads will roll. Even if they're made of stone."

I kind of wanted to applaud her for that line, but that would not endear us any more to Clare the gargoyle receptionist. She looked at us like we'd just announced we were planning to host a friendly football game between the vampires and the werewolves. "Feel free to ask her," she said, in grating tones. "We will send someone around to check your property shortly."

"I'll hold you to that," said Alissa.

Nothing to do but stick to our word, and release the wolves. I mean, Madame Grey. If she hadn't already been to the police station, she was presumably planning to march in with a plan.

"That was pretty amazing," I said to Alissa, as we walked towards the witches' main headquarters.

"I've been saving it up ever since she first handcuffed me at the hospital," she said.

"She did it? Not Steve?"

"They have a pack mentality. No wonder they get on

so well with the werewolves." She sighed. "Do you want to hold the fort while I tell Madame Grey? Because I wasn't exaggerating the *heads will roll* part. She'll clear out the whole house and probably assign us armed security." There was a pause. "Actually, you know, that might work out in your favour."

"Pfft. Nathan is too busy hunting for monsters in the woods," I said. "Besides, I don't think the person who left the flowers wanted to kill us. Just scare us, maybe."

"Yeah," she said. "The house is protected, which is probably why the spell didn't end up inside. It was triggered to go off when someone picked it up at the entrance. Where's Sky, anyway?"

"With his vampire friend," I said. "I think he and Vincent met at the bookshop before he even adopted me."

"Really? Oh, so that's why they get along so well."

"Yep. Someday I'm going to figure out how to get a straight answer out of a vampire."

"If anyone can, I guarantee Madame Grey will."

———

Madame Grey listened to our explanation with unnerving calmness. Her face betrayed nothing, but images of stormy skies filled my mind, and her wand glowed silver the whole time.

"Where are the flowers?" she asked.

"By the door to the house," said Alissa. "The spell's completely dead, but I can fetch them anyway, if it's possible to track who delivered them."

Madame Grey pinched the bridge of her nose. "The werewolves insist on a meeting to avoid bloodshed. I will send you adequate protection until I'm able to be there in person, and another witch will investigate the flowers and attempt to track down the person who sent them. Stay inside, and that includes your animals."

It looked like Sky's visits to the vampires' leader would have to be temporarily put on hold. Though I doubted even a locked door could stop my cat when he was on a mission.

"I have no control over that cat," I said. "But I'll try to."

"Good," she said. "Go home now, both of you. No detours. I will send your new security there shortly."

"I think she's going to send Nathan in," Alissa whispered to me, as Madame Grey's office door closed behind us.

"She'll have to fight the gargoyles first," I said. "And then she'll find out Steve dismissed you. I don't think I want to hang around for the fallout, to be honest."

"Me neither." She blew out a breath. "I need a distraction. Have you practised any magic with your left hand since you figured it out?"

"Nope. Didn't get the chance to tell Rita before she stuck me on theory work, and she hasn't been around since then. I'm up for some practise, but Madame Grey will make *our* heads roll if we knock the place down."

"Don't worry. I'm not letting you practise without a shield on the flat until you make it through a session without dying anything purple," she said, with a grin.

———

We entered the flat, where Roald lay snoozing on the sofa, next to Sky.

"There you have it," I said. "He has his own ways in and out of the house."

"Right..." Alissa kicked off her shoes, drew out her wand, then began setting up barriers on the room again in anticipation of my upcoming magical practise session. Hopefully this one would involve a little less paint.

My nerves, already jittery from our near-death experience, spiked. Alissa sat in the armchair, one leg crossed over the other. "Go on, Blair."

I retrieved my wand from my handbag. My skin tingled in anticipation, the small hairs on my arms standing on end.

"Which spell should I use?" I asked Alissa.

"Levitation," she said. "You always had trouble with that one, and I think it might be because your right hand made your aim lopsided."

I looked around for something safe to levitate—something not breakable. Not the glass on the coffee table, but there was a rolled-up magazine next to it. I took aim, and—

The coffee table rose into the air, its contents sliding alarmingly.

"Oh, no."

The sofa left the ground, too. Roald let out an indignant yowl, while Sky yawned and stretched, piercing me with a look as though he'd keep judging me intensely until I figured a way out of this mess.

"Blair, don't wave your wand around while you're thinking," Alissa said—too late. The chair she was sitting on went airborne. Then the bookcase.

"I'm not doing that!" I yelped. "It's like it's out of control. The house can't levitate... right?"

Her alarmed expression did not inspire confidence.

"Okay… spell reversal." I waved the wand in reverse at the table, and it slammed into the floor. By some miracle, the glass rolled onto the thick carpet and didn't smash.

The sofa wasn't so lucky. Roald leapt for cover in Alissa's arms as it hit the carpet hard enough to put a dent in the floorboards. I held my breath, certain we'd hear screaming from upstairs, but the wards Alissa had put on the room blocked out all sound, too.

Sky merely shook himself, hopped off the sofa, and carelessly padded over to the food bowl.

Alissa and I looked at one another. "I will never understand that cat as long as I live," I said.

"I don't understand your *magic*, Blair. I think you have an issue with moderation."

I looked at my wand hand. "You may be right."

"Don't use that again," she said. "Try smaller spells. Or… wait and tell Madame Grey. That's the sensible option."

I pulled a face. "Come on, I'm already housebound. Plus she'll be busy with the murders for the foreseeable future, or else stopping the werewolves and the vampires from going to war with one another."

"Good point. But I don't think antagonising the neighbours or the cats is a good move either. They're incarcerated along with us."

"Okay. Turn blue." I pointed at the cup, which turned from see-through to sky blue. "See, that one works. I guess I need to tighten my focus a little more."

The doorbell rang. I jumped, and the lights went out. "Ah." I didn't even know how I'd done that. I waved the wand again, casting the spell to summon light, and a dazzling array of rainbow lights exploded from the wand, floating up to the ceiling.

"Wow, that's pretty," Alissa said. The doorbell rang again. "I think it's my grandmother, or the person who's looking into who sent the flowers. Can you undo that spell?"

She ran to the door, while I held my wand hand still. The lights continued to blink overhead. *Er... I might need to look up the counter-spell.*

Alissa beckoned frantically. I left the lights and found it wasn't Madame Grey on the doorstep after all.

"Hey," Nathan said. "I guess I'm your security."

I stepped into the doorway to hide the flashing lights from view. "Madame Grey managed to persuade Steve to let you go?"

"Yes, she did." His gaze went to the lights still visible above my head. "What are you doing in there?"

"Causing chaos and destruction and annoying the cats. Er, Alissa, can you remember how to get rid of a bunch of lights?"

"That's all?" His eyes betrayed amusement. "That doesn't sound like a simple spell."

"It was supposed to be. I have no idea what's going on with my magic at the moment."

"You and me both." Alissa rolled her eyes. "I'll fix it. Put that wand of yours away, otherwise we'll be sending Nathan back to Madame Grey in pieces."

"I'm not *that* destructive." My face flushed like a furnace. "My magic is a little out of control, though."

"Any reason?" He looked at the wand in my hand.

Oh, there was no harm in telling him. "I just found out my wand only works in my left hand. I can't explain why.

I'm right-handed. And it's also a little volatile. The slightest movement makes things like that happen." The lights flashed again, proving my point.

"Really?" He eyed my left hand. "Did that come up in your lessons?"

"I haven't even had the chance to ask Rita or Madame Grey, but it explains why I've been so slow to grasp basic spells. I do know the theory. So Alissa and I are practising."

"Or one of us is heading for cover," said Alissa, reappearing behind me. "I got rid of the lights. How did you even do that?"

"I have no idea," I said. "It's like there's a disconnect between my wand and my brain."

"You need to learn the reverse of the wands' movements," Alissa said. "Because it's your left hand. I guess you got lucky with that first spell."

"I also used a summoning one," I said, thinking of the hummingbird-thing at work. "Okay. I should tell Madame Grey, but now she has angry gargoyles to deal with as well as werewolves."

"She doesn't seem bothered by the gargoyles," said Nathan. "She claimed sorting them out will be simple."

"Steve is like an annoying fly who won't go away," said Alissa. "Not so much the werewolves. I gathered she planned to knock a few heads together."

"It looked that way," commented Nathan. "She also told me of her intent to escalate your police report on the attack."

"Yeah, she planned to have someone check the flowers," I said.

"When I met her, she said they found no conclusive

results," said Nathan. "Do either of you have any clues about who might have sent the spell?"

"I thought Bryan, but he doesn't want to hurt Alissa," I said. "Unless he *is* an accomplice, but I can't see what he'd get out of killing his fellow werewolves."

"He wouldn't," Alissa said firmly. "I know that much about him, unless he's really gone off the rails lately. There's nothing to gain from taking me out of the picture, other than ticking off Madame Grey."

"Unless… I was the target," I said. "I've spoken to several of the suspects, right? Well, the vampires, anyway."

"Tell me who you've spoken to," Nathan said. "I'll make a list."

"Lord Anderson, Peter, Bryan… and all the vampires who were trying to get into Lord Goddard's house will have seen me helping Madame Grey. Oh, and Vincent, but he doesn't want me dead. But all of those people have more or less said they aren't the killer."

"The killer might indeed have accomplices," Nathan said. "I'll be outside your house until I do my rounds of the forest. Madame Grey thinks I should check your mail during the day. Nothing odd has happened at night, has it?"

No. Aside from glitter and pixie dust.

"No," I said. "Nothing at all. Nobody has made any threats or anything. I've felt as safe as ever walking around town."

"Or maybe you were targeted without knowing it," he said, not fooled for an instant. "I understand that you feel you have an obligation to help, but now the situation has escalated, it's simply too dangerous to carry on as before."

My heart sank. "But—I can't just wait here for the

killer to show up. Two people are already dead. Three, if the elf is connected as well. This isn't just about me. And if the killer is someone I've already spoken to, I have to figure out who it is."

"Then you'll go nowhere alone," he said. "Madame Grey's orders, not mine."

Alissa didn't look too happy, either. "Bryan will clam up if he comes under questioning," she said. "I'm going to give him a text and ask to speak to him in person. Nobody else has ever left me flowers. He tried to do the same in the hospital."

The hospital. Wait a moment.

"Back in a second," I said to Nathan, and closed the door to our flat. "Poisoned… flowers. Alissa, do you have that reference book?"

"Which one?"

I ran back into the flat—thankfully, the disco lights had gone—and scanned the piles of witch textbooks on the shelf. I still had the book I'd used to look up the leaves of the plant used to poison Mr Bayer, months ago. And the victims had died by poisoning. Hemlock… definitely wasn't bright purple flowers, but they were distinctive enough to send alarm bells ringing in my head.

I paused on the correct entry in the book. The bright purple flowers in the picture matched the ones we'd found outside.

The flowers were known to be poisonous to fairies. I'd been the target, not Alissa.

I let the book fall onto the table, dread coursing through me. The person who'd left the flowers knew I was a fairy. Who? Was it the same person who'd killed the vampire and the werewolf, or was someone else responsible?

Too many people might know the truth now. Any vampire could have read it from my mind in the time I'd been helping Madame Grey try to disable the wards around Lord Goddard's house. Lord Anderson had implied he knew, but he might not have done. Maybe he was just warning me off generally, not because he thought I'd be a particular target. On the other hand, he'd certainly seemed to have a specific interest in me. And bite marks connected the two deaths. He'd even been a suspect in the first murder.

I jumped when the doorbell rang again. "Nathan?"

Alissa's jaw clenched as she looked at her phone. "Bryan. I told him to call me, not come here." She composed herself, then walked to the door. I followed closely behind.

Bryan stood on the doorstep, his head drooped. Nathan had stepped aside, but clearly had no intention of moving to give him space to talk to Alissa.

"Come to explain yourself?" she asked.

"I didn't do it," he rasped. He looked downcast, his eyes shadowed. "I swear, I didn't mean to hurt anyone, least of all you."

Alissa blew out a breath. "I won't lie, it looks bad for you. You're the only person who's made a habit of leaving flowers out here for the world to see."

He shook his head, backing away from her glare. "I just came here to explain. I didn't—I'm not with the killer. Whoever it is."

"Tell that to Madame Grey," said Alissa.

He blanched. "She knows the werewolves have no argument with the witches."

"No, just the vampires," I said. *And the fairies?* But he was one of the few people who *hadn't* read that particular piece of information from my head. So how could he have known? Or had it been a coincidence? The spell had been intended to knock someone out, not kill. The poison wasn't as obvious and common as hemlock, unless he'd known the flowers were deadly to fairies.

"Believe me," he said, "I wish we didn't have an argument with them, either. They've lost someone, too. I think there's one killer, and it's a rogue."

"A rogue what, exactly?" Nathan asked.

Bryan frowned. "What're you doing here?"

"I'm watching out for any potential enemies," he said.

"Including the killer and their accomplices. If I were you, I'd be very careful what you say."

Bryan doesn't know my ability. None of his words had registered as lies, either.

Bryan took a step away from the door. "Sorry. I shouldn't have come. Just thought I'd give an explanation. Er, I don't think that vampire did it either."

Alissa's eyes narrowed. "Why come to see me in the hospital, then? Was that for the same reason?"

He shook his head. "No, I... I don't have a chance with you, do I?"

"You seriously only just figured that out? I think you should leave."

"I agree," said Nathan, taking a deliberate step in Bryan's direction.

Bryan gave Alissa one last pleading look, then sloped away.

Alissa groaned. "No lies, right, Blair?"

"None," I said in a low voice. "Except for lying by omission, maybe. But I don't think he did it."

Nathan turned to me. "Do you have a theory?"

Yeah, but it sounds paranoid. I wouldn't have known the flowers were poisonous to fairies if I hadn't had access to that book. It didn't seem common knowledge. Right? Vampires knew fairies, if Lord Goddard was any indication, but I really didn't want to have that conversation with Nathan now.

"Lord Anderson," I said. "The first vampire we spoke to. Given the bite marks on the latest victim, I think it's probably safe to say it's a vampire. He was a suspect in Lord Goddard's murder—not to mention he seemed to be interested in me. That's the connecting factor."

Nathan's brow pinched. "Perhaps."

There was also the fact that I'd blocked his mind control. But that was after the murder, and he clearly hadn't been prepared for me to do that. Maybe that's why he'd tried to attack me, but he'd had the chance to incapacitate Nathan and take me down at any point when we'd been near his house. Nathan was armed and experienced, but you couldn't outdo a vampire for speed. The town's security rules depended on the vampires playing by their own rulebook. When that went out the window… who knew what would happen?

"I don't know about confronting him on his own territory this time," I admitted. "I almost want to go through Vincent again, because the only person who can really bring down a vampire is another vampire. I don't know. The facts fit. But he didn't lie."

"He won't hurt you," Nathan said. "Not if we meet him on neutral territory. I can get a warrant from Madame Grey to speak to him again. He's still technically on the police's suspect list, and the attempt against the two of you makes him more suspicious by default. Unless you have any other theories?"

"The wizard," I said. "Peter. I know he said he'd leave the wards down, but the house re-sealed itself again. I saw when I was on the way to the vampires' place to speak to Vincent."

"You went back to the vampires again?" asked Nathan.

"I thought Vincent might be able to help Keith. Instead, I found my cat."

"Madame Grey specifically asked me to warn you not to wander outside alone, certainly not to the vampires' territory or the forest," he said. "If you want to meet with the suspects again, I'd be happy to go with you, but I'd advise you against going anywhere unaccompanied as long as this killer is on the loose. I'm sorry if that sounds patronising, but—"

"Vampires are dangerous. Got it." I didn't want to argue with him, so I said, "I do think we ought to talk to the suspects again, and see if there's anything we missed. Any idea why Peter decided to lock his house up again?"

"I would guess that it's because he left town," Nathan said. "According to the police, anyway. The gargoyles said he packed up and left in the middle of the night."

"Seriously?" I said. "Well, I don't think he was involved. It was just bad luck that the vampire put that curse on his house so nobody but him can get in. On the other hand, he's also our only means of getting into the house if Lord Goddard left any clues behind that we missed the first time around. Did nobody see where he went?"

"No. He left no note, in case the vampires followed," Nathan said.

"I guess I don't really blame him." I didn't think we'd missed anything at the house—aside from that pixie, and I was so sure I'd seen it in the garden since. Given the poisonous flowers, maybe it was for the best that it hadn't stuck around, but I wished I knew how it all connected.

"I'm going to clean up the mess I made when I cast a levitation charm," I said to Nathan. "Let us know when Madame Grey shows up, okay?"

Alissa raised her eyebrows at me when I closed the door. "I wouldn't have stood in your way if you two wanted to chat." She made quotation marks with her fingers on the last word.

I swatted at her. "That's not it. This is serious." I

crossed the room to where I'd dropped the book. "Look at this."

She blinked at the purple flowers. "Yeah, those are the flowers someone booby-trapped. I know. Why?"

"They're poisonous to fairies."

Her mouth opened in an *o*. "Are you sure? I had no clue, and I studied poisons."

I closed the book. "Might be a coincidence, might not, but it explains why the pixie never came back."

She blinked. "Pixie?"

"There was a pixie in Lord Goddard's house. I assume they were friends, like Vincent and my cat. It's not like I can ask him now he's dead. But I also saw it in our garden in the middle of the night the other day. It disappeared when I tried to chase it. At least, I'm pretty sure I wasn't dreaming."

"Here?" Alissa's brows rose. "You're being followed by a pixie?"

"Possibly. I don't even know." I tossed the book onto the coffee table. "Maybe the killer sent the flowers intending to poison me, maybe not, but half the suspects know what I am."

"They do? The vampires… does the wizard?"

"I think so, but I doubt he's coming back, thanks to those vampires. It's that other vampire, Lord Anderson, I should have spoken to. Nathan's going to ask if we can go and question him again."

"Right." She nodded. "Now my grandmother is directly involved, the investigation should be much smoother."

"And—Keith? Is she going to help him get out of jail?"

She dropped her gaze. "There's not much she can do if it looks like he's guilty. It's unjust. Believe me, there are things I'd like to say to those gargoyles, but I'm not the one with the power here. If they set off my grandmother, though…"

"Heads will roll. Let's just hope she's the one to do it, and not the werewolves."

———

That night, my dreams were even more intense than before. Vivid images of flying, above a forest, the wind rustling my wings. *My wings.*

I should have felt free, but there was something chasing me, something dangerous…

"MIAOW."

I yelped and fell off the bed. Sky stood upright on the windowsill, hissing angrily. I jumped upright and ran to the window, peering out into the night, but there was nobody there.

"What?" I lifted Sky off the windowsill, where he promptly ran to my bed and sprawled where I'd been lying. "Oh, come on."

The cat yawned.

"Some familiar you are." I checked the time, and picked up my wand. I had a magic lesson this evening after work, assuming Rita didn't cancel on me again and nobody else got murdered. That was a cheery thought. Maybe it was for the best I wasn't playing the part of the smiling receptionist at Dritch & Co full time.

The smell of herbal tea drifted from the kitchen, filling the air with its calming scent. I found Alissa stirring a mug of a calming draught, and helped myself to one of my own. Her eyes were underscored with dark circles and her nails bitten down to the quick. I wasn't the only one who'd had a restless night. With her vampire friend in jail, it wasn't surprising.

"Nathan's not outside," she said, checking her phone. "I think he's still in the forest."

"They're going to have to let him sleep at some point." Not that I felt particularly well-rested. What did these dreams mean? Sometimes they felt distant, like memories. Other times they were more nightmare material. And no pixie had materialised. Given the fairy poison, though, I doubted I'd be seeing it again anytime soon. "And hire more people," I added, taking a seat at the table.

"They have." She yawned. "The gargoyles have taken to the skies. Swooping around looking for trouble. Still managed to miss the latest."

I dropped my spoon. "Latest?"

"Another body in the woods, Madame Grey said. I guess that's what Nathan's dealing with."

My stomach turned over. "Another elf?"

"I assumed so," said Alissa, sitting at the breakfast table opposite me. "Not a werewolf, anyway, though they're still all fired up over the last one. Nobody's declared war yet."

"Just what I want to wake up to in the morning." I sipped my tea, wishing I'd opted for motivational coffee instead so I wouldn't fall asleep at work today. "Does Madame Grey have an update on who's due for a questioning next?"

"Nope. I'll keep you posted. I'm working this morning, but I'll be free in the afternoon. They won't let me into Keith's questioning one way or another. I just wish I could help him."

"Hmm." I tugged a hand through my hair. "Ever get the feeling the person who planted that spell wanted to actively stop us from involving ourselves in the investigation? If they'd wanted to kill us in person, they might have done it at any time. Me, certainly, with all the running around I did."

"Perhaps they couldn't catch you on those boots."

"Ha." I took another sip of tea, its warmth somewhat soothing my nerves. "Yeah, right. All they'd need to do was put an obstacle in the way and I'd fall straight onto my face."

"Or send in Nathan."

"I don't think our date's happening, somehow."

And my magic lesson? I didn't care if the werewolves, vampires or otherwise stood in my way: I'd tell Madame Grey what was going on with my magic, and I'd get some answers. Target or not, the killer was linked to me in some way. And if nobody solved the case, the town's peace might be shattered forever.

12

I got through work on caffeine and persistence, throwing myself into every task to avoid thinking of the murders and the most recent attempt on my life. The others in the office seemed reluctant to chat, too, while Veronica remained shut in her office with a 'Do not disturb: chimera feeding in progress' sign on the door. I hadn't even told her about my recent discoveries about my magic, but I wasn't about to see if there actually was a chimera in there. Bethan said her mother was paranoid about security but couldn't get Madame Grey to allow anyone else to come and help. The pack refused to let Callie out of their sight, while Nathan was surrounded by people desperate to hire a paranormal hunter to protect them from rampaging werewolves and murderous vampires.

I got out of work as soon as the day ended. The instant I arrived home, I'd be under watch, which gave me a few minutes to do as much poking around as possible before someone realised I wasn't where I was supposed to be.

141

Hurrying down the high street, I made straight for the bookshop. I'd get more out of snooping through Madame Grey's books, but she didn't have any volumes on fairies, to my knowledge. I might know the flowers were poisonous to me, but maybe there was another fairy-related clue I'd missed. Or at least a clue that explained why that pixie had shown up in a dead vampire's house and then followed me.

I wove through the shelves to the section where I'd found the general guide to fairies I'd looked at the first time I'd come here. I skimmed through the list that unfurled when I tapped the button on the shelf, but when I reached the spot where the *Guide to Fairies and Other Species* should be, it no longer showed up as listed. I checked the shelf, but it wasn't there. Someone else must have bought it, and the shop had had only the one copy.

Maybe I'm not the only one with an academic interest in fairies. Had Madame Grey or one of the witches had taken it out? A fair few people knew my hybrid nature by now, which made it all the more difficult to figure out if the flowers had been intended for me, or the perpetrator hadn't known they were poisonous. Especially as their positioning had indicated the flowers were for Alissa, not me. Nathan had left me bubble wrap, not flowers.

Chatter from the cafe at the back reached my ears, reminding me of the 'date' Nathan and I had been on during my first week in town—when Blythe had hidden somewhere behind one of these bookshelves and cast a spell on me to make me fall on my face. I turned around, suddenly conscious that I was ignoring Madame Grey's request to stay out of danger, but saw nobody except a few casual browsers. Dropping my hand to the shelf's edge, I hit the button to make the list of titles on the shelves too high to reach appear. The list unfurled almost to my feet, showing me all manner of eclectic magical titles.

Wood Fairies and their Relations. I tapped the list and the book leapt into my hand. The textbook mostly seemed to be about elves, but I did find a section on pixies near the back.

According to the book, pixies were fairly simple creatures which loved practical jokes. They weren't intelligent fairies, but were more so than your average cat... somehow, I thought Sky would find that insulting.

Speaking of Sky. He'd lived here before, in the bookshop, before he'd come to find me. He'd also, if my eyes hadn't deceived me, had been able to see through the pixie's glamour.

I skipped ahead in the book, to the glossary. I ran my finger down the list, and my gaze snagged on *fairy cats.*

Fairy cats.

I stared at the words. *No way.*

Skipping to the relevant section, I paused. *Fairy cats are highly intelligent creatures that are typically independent and self-sufficient. While most shun humans, it is not unheard of for a fairy cat to develop a friendship with another paranormal who it chooses to be its special companion.*

The description fitted Sky so well, I had to reread it a couple of times to check I hadn't made it all up. Maybe he'd picked me because I was a fairy—not because he was a witch's cat and witches needed familiars, but because he'd felt some kinship with me.

I returned my attention to the book. The description didn't mention anything about mind-reading, but Sky's link with the vampires must be one-sided. When Vincent had asked him to fetch me to help Alissa, he must have used his own psychic power to project the image at him. Fairy cats could pick up on things nobody else could. And as to how he'd got into the flat when all the windows were closed? The book said that fairy cats weren't a hundred percent understood, since they generally avoided people, but had been known to show up in locked rooms or places that nobody should be able to get into.

I lowered the book when a couple of other customers moved to browse nearby, and returned it to the shelf to avoid drawing attention. I might not have any leads on the killer, but now I might understand my cat a little better.

I walked out of the shop, grateful for the crowded high street for making me feel slightly more secure walking to my magic lesson alone. The town still felt safe, the faces familiar, and I hated the idea of there being someone among them who meant me harm.

I entered the witches' headquarters and found Rita in the entrance hall, a bundle of books in her arms.

"Blair?" she said. "What are you doing here?"

"I know I'm early for my lesson," I said, "but I have something important to tell you. About my magic."

To my relief, she nodded and opened the door to the classroom. I scooted in ahead of her, and when the door was closed, I explained. Quickly. Her brows rose when I told her how I'd accidentally made a dent in the floor with the sofa. Not to mention the disco lights display.

"No, reverse wand holding isn't common at all," she

said. "One in a thousand, if that."

"Is it because I'm half fairy? Weird stuff has been going on with my magic for a while now. Even with my wand in my left hand, I'm having trouble with moderation. When I lifted the sofa, it was only supposed to levitate a rolled-up newspaper."

She nodded. "It's entirely possible your two magical types are clashing in some manner. I do want to apologise for the situation you're in. I know it isn't easy. But you've been made into a target, and—the last thing Madame Grey and I want is to lose you. Our own attachments aside, there are others to consider—and your family."

My family.

There was a time and a place to keep secrets, and this wasn't it. Not when I may have been targeted for my fairy nature alone.

I took in a deep breath, and told her about the note.

"I didn't go," I finished. "Obviously, going to the falls in the middle of the night is a bad idea at the best of times. But the body showed up, and I didn't want to risk it. Ever since then, I've been having… nightmares. About being a fairy."

"Tell me about these dreams."

I gave her a brief rundown. "Flying, mostly. Being chased. Sometimes I'm looking into a mirror, and I'm not —human."

Her lips pursed. "I'm a diviner, not a seer… there's a difference there. Dreams such as yours can mean a great many things. You might be remembering the past. Or you might be worried for the future."

I didn't need a crystal ball to tell me *that.*

"It might be that after your glamour came off, the

memories started to come back, but they sound too vivid to be your own childhood memories. How long have you been in foster care?"

"My whole life, as far as I know," I said. "But Mr and Mrs Wilkes took me in when I was three. They haven't lied to me and they aren't magical."

"No," she said. "I'd advise you to put it out of mind, if you can. Your witch magic sounds like it's the part that needs work on, and it's certainly the only part I can personally help you with."

She wasn't wrong. I wasn't sure if I actually felt any better, when it came down to it, after telling her. But it was nice to know that I wasn't entirely alone.

"To be honest, it feels like even my witch magic is spinning out of control," I admitted. "Sometimes I wave my wand and it does what it's supposed to, but other times, it levitates everything in the room. It might even have levitated the house if I'd kept going. It doesn't seem to have an 'off' switch."

"Magic often reacts to strong emotions," she said. "Is your paranormal-sensing power behaving as it normally would?"

"Same as ever," I answered. "But… well. I accidentally blocked a vampire from reading my mind the other day. Maybe two. I'm not sure how I did it. Does that ability definitely come from my mother's side of the family?"

She pursed her lips. "I would imagine so, given your mother's gift, but she definitely wasn't able to block vampires' mind-reading skills. I'd suggest asking Madame Grey about that development."

"Might have to wait a while," I said wryly. "I know she's busy dealing with the werewolves. But I can't pick up my wand without it dying things purple at the moment, and I'd really like to know why."

"If you like, I can take it off your hands," she said.

"Best not," I said. "Considering everything that's happened, it might well save my life."

Her gaze became shadowed. "I wish I didn't think you were right."

Considering someone had tried to poison me... no wonder Sky hadn't been near the flat when the flowers had been planted there. Since he hadn't warned me, I could only assume he hadn't been present.

"There's another thing," I said to her. "My cat. I think he's a fairy cat. I just went to the bookshop on the way back from work, and I picked up a book on fairy creatures. Sky fits the description. Can't explain why he makes friends with vampires, but the two of us have never entirely connected in the way a witch and her familiar should be."

She arched a brow. "Fairy cats? Hmm. I can't say I've ever met one before. Did you say... makes friends with vampires?"

"He and Vincent are buddies," I said. "They knew each other before Sky found me. But we've never seen eye to eye. Maybe it's because he thinks I'm basically human..."

"Human," she said. "You've never taken off your glamour?"

"I can't do it myself," I admitted. "But—the waterfall can temporarily remove glamour. I haven't been able to go there since the murders, but..."

"Yes?"

I dropped my gaze. "The flowers that were left at my flat are poisonous to fairies."

"Goddess," she said. "Have you told Madame Grey?"

I shook my head. "I realised last night. She's been occupied all day, and I might be wrong. I mean, it's not common knowledge that they're deadly to fairies, let alone that I'm half of one."

"Unless the spell was meant to divert your attention," she said. "Did the person responsible expect you to think the flowers were a gift from Nathan?"

"I wondered, but he's never left me flowers. Alissa's ex has. She wasn't home when they were left there, though. She was at the jail arguing with the gargoyles on Keith's behalf."

She looked at me, in such a way that suggested she was looking right into my thoughts. "You do have a theory, Blair, don't you?"

"Lord Anderson," I said. "He was the first suspect, and he asked to speak to me in particular when I didn't even know him. At first, I thought it was because he wanted me to use my lie-sensing ability to get him off the hook. But if he's working with someone else who's committing the murders, he'd be able to honestly answer my questions and not give the game away."

"And you think he tried to scare you off when you became involved in the case?" she asked.

"Maybe. The spell was intended to knock out, not kill. We know the killer at least has a vampire accomplice, since there were bite marks on one of the victims."

"Logical thinking," she said. "However, that doesn't explain the other murders in the woods."

"Another elf was found, right?" I asked. "Yeah, I heard. I'm not sure how the monster attacks link to the murders, but I do think Lord Anderson is involved in some way. At this point, he looks the guiltiest of everyone I've spoken to."

I was sure I was right… but who was killing the elves? A vampire would have no reason to set monsters loose when they came equipped with sharp teeth of their own.

"I see," she said. "Have you told the police this?"

"Nathan was going to," I said. "But I can't see an elder vampire submitting to being jailed without a fuss, nor the gargoyles pulling their usual interrogation tactics on him. Do they even account for the fact that vampires can pluck their questions from their minds before they even speak aloud?"

"No, unfortunately," she said. "But the werewolves are still at the police station. If they figure out your theory…"

"They might strike first." I nodded. "Yeah. That's what I'm afraid of. This requires a delicate hand, and nobody has one of those. Including me. I don't know if the police really think that Keith did it, either. I think he's innocent. But my word isn't enough for them, even though he directly said he didn't do it. On the other hand, so did Bryan."

She seemed to turn this over in her mind. "I'll speak to Madame Grey. As for you, I'd suggest you go home."

Dismissed again. I was far from in the mood for magical lessons, and after the latest revelation, I was a little concerned for my cat. On the other hand, Alissa would be working right now. I wished I'd had the chance to look around the hospital, but with gargoyles at every corner, I shouldn't push my luck.

I left the building—and stopped, staring ahead. Two people walked past, one of them moving with the grace and swiftness of a vampire.

The other was Nathan.

I remained still, my gaze following them. They leaned closer to one another as though conversing in conspiratorial whispers. Uneasiness stirred within me. That wasn't Vincent. It was Lord Anderson. The man I suspected must be the killer.

I'd told Nathan I suspected that guy. Why was he hanging around with a murder suspect?

He must be questioning him. Of course he wouldn't trust the police to handle the matter, but talking to him in public seemed odd. Let alone walking together through town, conversing in low whispers like old friends. Something in their manner bothered me, not least the fact that Nathan had implied he'd let me talk to Lord Anderson in person, as long as he went with me.

I hung back, debating. On the one hand, Lord Anderson would clam up the instant he saw me if he really was the killer. On the other hand, I was the one with the ability to sense lies, and I couldn't hear a word they said. I wished I'd looked up an eavesdropping spell or something similar, but there was no time.

I cast my mind around for the spells I'd memorised. The *hidden* spell might do the trick. It was a basic spell that witches and wizards used when they went to a normal town or city, like a simple version of the wards that kept the town hidden. I pulled out my wand, and waved it carefully. While I didn't turn purple or start flashing with disco lights, the only way to really test the spell was to walk directly in front of someone and see if they noticed. Unfortunately, Nathan was trained to see through disguises, and vampires' enhanced senses mean there was a strong chance it wouldn't work on him, but I could at least follow closely behind them without being seen.

Their path turned off the high street, and continued towards the forest.

I switched on the levitating boots, more to stop myself from tripping than anything else. If I'd been alone, this wouldn't be a smart move, but I trusted Nathan. Even if walking into a forest alone with a vampire was the sort of thing he'd tell *me* not to do.

I followed them down the path, hoping that the general forest noise would stop the vampire's enhanced hearing from picking up on me, while Nathan would be too preoccupied to look behind him for Blair-shaped shadows.

"The elves aren't here," Nathan said in a low voice.

"They're not pleased," said the vampire. "They might be quiet, but they will not forgive whoever trespassed on their territory."

He doesn't know, then?

"No," said Nathan. "I suppose not. Do you think the werewolves plan to attack the vampires before the case draws to a conclusion?"

Hearing those words from Nathan's mouth turned my blood to ice.

"Maybe they will," the vampire murmured. "Perhaps we will get to the bottom of this sorry case and there will be no need for panic at all."

He slipped away with vampire grace, leaving me staring at Nathan's back.

What did he mean by that? Was Lord Anderson not guilty after all? But if so, who else might have left the flowers?

I didn't bother with stealth. I remained standing there on the path while Nathan turned back to retrace his steps, and folded my arms. "Care to tell me what that was about?"

13

I wished I could read lies from Nathan's expression as easily as his words, because he wasn't saying any at the moment. His mouth pressed together. "Blair," he said. "You shouldn't be in here."

"Please tell me that wasn't what it looked like," I said.

"What did it look like?"

"Are you kidding me?" I said. "He—you know I had him listed as a suspect. The person who tried to kill me. Why talk to him alone? What did he say to you?"

He looked drained. If I didn't know better, I'd say a vampire had taken a bite out of him. I surreptitiously looked at his neck, just in case.

"What is it, Blair?" he asked.

"Just checking for bite marks," I said. "That, or you've been replaced by an impostor. What were you doing with him?"

"Discussing the case," he said.

"In the forest?" I waved a hand to indicate the trees. "The same forest you found two dead bodies in—three, if you count the werewolf. And where another vampire was bitten by an unknown assailant."

"I thought it best to get his side of the explanation, somewhere we wouldn't be confronted."

"What *is* his side?"

"He's not the killer, Blair."

"Then who?" I queried. "He fits the description. He's on the suspect list, he's a vampire, he's read my thoughts and—" *He knows I'm a fairy.*

"He's concerned about the potential war with the werewolves," Nathan said.

"Did you not think it suspicious that he and Lord Goddard were rivals before he died, and he asked to speak to me in person like he was desperate to cover his traces? We know there's a vampire involved in this. Even if you discount the fact that the werewolf victim had bite marks on him, Keith got attacked in this very forest, by a rogue who still hasn't been caught yet."

"I know the vampires haven't helped their own case," said Nathan. "But it was Lord Anderson who stopped the other vampires from swarming the wizard's house."

"I think he might have been a little too late with that," I said. "The wizard's gone, and if the vampire isn't guilty... who did it?"

He shook his head. "I don't know. I'm no more of a detective than you are, Blair. Does Madame Grey know you're here?"

I blew out a frustrated breath. "No. Come on, I saw the guy I like walking into the forest with a vampire I thought was the person who tried to kill me the other day. You can't blame me for getting a bit suspicious."

His expression softened. "No, I don't fault your inquisitiveness. It's one of the reasons I was drawn to you to begin with."

"What, when I was lost and wandering around the lake?" I said. *I miss that.* Not the confusion, but that weird sense of security that had pervaded ever since I'd arrived in Fairy Falls. Even now, the forest hinted at tranquillity, from the faint rustling noises to the subtle smells of the flowers witches gathered to use in their potions. It just seemed unfair that one person could undo all that peace virtually overnight.

Nathan took a step towards me. "Absolutely. Are we still on for our date on Friday?"

"Assuming no more bodies show up and we don't wake up to vampires and werewolves at each other's throats? Sure." Despite my utter exhaustion and frustration, maybe we could temporarily put all this behind us. "But Madame Grey practically has me under house arrest, and you're pretty much in agreement with her."

He raised an eyebrow. "You seem to have dodged her relatively easily."

"I'm going to get into trouble for this, and you know it. I figured that even if Lord Anderson was the villain, you're the one person I wouldn't mind having around in a creepy forest."

"Thanks. I think." He smiled briefly. "I'll walk you home. Is Alissa at the hospital?"

"Yeah, I was going to meet her after her shift finished."

"Then we'll head there, to make sure both of you get home safely."

"Yeah." *But she's not the target. I am.* Secrets writhed inside my chest like a nest of serpents, but who might be listening out here? Vampires—like the one who'd disappeared into the woods yet moved swiftly as smoke on the breeze. Maybe it was for the best that I had a bodyguard. I found myself relieved that we hadn't gone that far into the woods. Though Nathan's insistence that Lord Anderson was innocent put my theories about the murderer back at square one.

The gargoyle security guard at the hospital gave me an accusing stare as I walked up to the doors. "Your friend just left," he growled. "If you keep disobeying the orders of your superiors, you'll be lucky to last out the week."

I rolled my eyes, turning my back on the gargoyle. "Nice. I didn't think the gargoyles were invested in my well-being."

"If Madame Grey's calling the shots with the police, it can only be a good thing," Nathan commented.

"Better hope she can talk the werewolves out of going to war."

There was a pause. "It's speculation," he said. "I asked Lord Anderson because I wanted a vampire's viewpoint on the issue, but as long as the werewolves don't push the vampires into outright conflict, the situation shouldn't escalate."

So he knew I'd been eavesdropping on him and Lord Anderson... and more to the point, while his words hadn't exactly set off my inner lie detector, they did give off a vibe that wasn't entirely truthful, and he didn't quite meet my eyes.

"I can't blame you for getting curious," he said. "But I wish you'd consider your safety."

"I am. So is everyone else." I indicated the gargoyle's hulking form outside the hospital. "Anyway, what about *your* safety?"

"Mine? I know the forest like the back of my hand, and I've dealt with most paranormal creatures at some time or other."

"Doesn't mean you know what this one is, right?" I scanned his face for clues. "Why didn't you ask me to speak to Lord Anderson? You knew I wanted to."

I didn't want to argue with him, but the presence of the gargoyle close behind was a reminder that despite his obvious concern for me, he and the witches would happily wrap me in bubble wrap until the case was done. And until then? Bye, bye, freedom.

"Never mind," I said, ducking my head. "Forget I asked."

Mostly, I didn't want to listen to him lie.

I hurried the rest of the way home, and found Alissa unlocking the door. "You look like Sky put mice in your underwear drawer again," she said.

"I think I wrecked things with Nathan," I said quietly. "He was with Lord Anderson. You know, the guy I thought was the culprit."

Her eyes widened. "What? Seriously?"

"Yep. He thinks the guy's innocent. If anyone other than you or him had said so, or maybe Madame Grey, I wouldn't believe them. We're looking for a rogue vampire. One with a personal interest in me, if I was the target."

"And if not?" She walked ahead of me into the flat. "I think the intention was to get the two of us out of the investigation. We weren't the original targets."

I chewed on my lower lip. "I just wish I knew how it all fit together. The werewolf got bitten before he died. The vampire died by a method that's likely to have been used by another vampire. The elves were probably attacked by an animal. Maybe our villain's pet. That, or he's trying to keep people out of the forest because he's hiding in there."

"Er, wasn't Nathan wandering around the forest anyway? Not to mention the werewolves, or elves. Otherwise I'd say you had a point."

"Right, but the killer uses poison. They might also have bitten Keith. I mean, he was in the forest. Maybe he saw something. I doubt being in jail is helping."

As her face fell, I wished I hadn't spoken.

"Yeah," she said. "Believe me, the hospital nearly kicked me off my shift early because I kept texting my grandmother and leaving messages for the police, too. They're not going to get any answers out of him using intimidation."

"Doesn't look like Keith is getting a questioning at all. I can't believe I told Nathan that I suspected the vampire of murder and then he went and made friends with him."

"Somehow I doubt that's what's going on."

"It's frustrating, whatever it is," I said. "I trust Nathan. I hate that he seems to think it's his duty to keep me out of harm's way by not getting me involved at all."

"Wait, aren't you supposed to be going on a date with him on Friday?"

I dug my hands in my pockets. "Yep. Apparently, we're still on, but given what Madame Grey is like at the moment, I'm not sure she'll let me. *And* I'm still keeping secrets from him. So having a go at him for being less than truthful is going to backfire in my face when he finds out."

"You're not wrong."

I gave her an eye-roll. "I know, I know. I'll tell him on

our date. Assuming Madame Grey doesn't send us an armed escort."

Alissa said, "How do you know she won't?"

Oh, no.

———

"This," I said, "is not a date. By any stretch of the imagination."

Nathan and I sat uncomfortably at the central table in the Troll's Tavern on Friday night. Most of the other tables were empty. Witches milled around, not even bothering to hide that they had their wands primed for action. There was also a gargoyle outside, who'd glowered at me when Nathan and I had walked in. Two witches stood in the corner, occasionally casting a tracking spell over the whole bar to light up the whole place and turf out any potential lurkers. Nobody was using the pool tables.

Everyone who came in either left immediately, or picked a table in the centre. Hence our positioning. Dating should not take place under a spotlight with armed security. Especially when the person I was dating *was* security.

"This is unnecessary," I added, when Nathan didn't respond. Neither of us had done much more than pick at our food. He looked tired enough to pass out in his beer glass. "Just how much did all these people cost to hire?"

"Less than the guards outside your house."

"That doesn't make me feel better." I pushed my mostly-full plate aside and took a sip of cocktail in the hope that it'd banish my bad mood. "Maybe we should have done this another time. This isn't the place for a private chat, either."

"It could be. There are spells."

"Privacy spells?" I grabbed my wand and accidentally turned the ceiling transparent. A dozen witches immediately jumped in to correct my mistake, their wands moving fast enough to make my hair stand on end.

"Can we help you with anything?" asked one of them, a pink-haired witch.

I felt kind of bad for being so annoyed with them. They likely hadn't been given much of a choice when Madame Grey had pressured them to follow us on our date. "Privacy," I said. "I take it we aren't going to be allowed to walk home alone."

"We'll keep a respectable distance, Miss Wilkes."

"Not for making out," I accidentally said aloud. Oops. I reeled my voice into calmness. "Er. I mean, we actually want to discuss something important where nobody else can overhear."

"If you desire," said the witch.

She waved her wand, and I turned to Nathan, blushing to the tips of my ears. *Not for making out.* Great one there, Blair.

"Not that I don't want to make out with you," I blurted. "Just not—I mean the appropriate time—"

"Don't worry about it," he cut in. "What did you want to talk about?"

I grimaced. "If this is what dating you is going to be like, I think I'll stick to spending all my spare time with my cat."

"I did want to be here, Blair."

My muscles turned to jelly. *Go on. Tell him.*

"I have something to tell you," I squeaked. "I'm really sorry I didn't say sooner, but—"

Sparks shot from my wand, which I'd stashed in my pocket. "Ah."

No sound came out of my mouth. My wand had gone off… and cast a silencing spell.

I pulled the wand out, and all the glasses on the bar turned into toads. Croaking filled the pub, while the witches hastened to undo the damage with such efficiency that I kind of wanted to order them to go after the killer instead of wasting their time guarding me. Finally, my voice—and Nathan's—came back.

"I'm sorry!" I said. "Honestly. My magic is out of control. And that's what I wanted to talk to you about. I'm sorry I didn't tell you before, but I'm a fa—"

He wasn't looking at me, but at his phone. "I've been called out," he said. "Another body in the woods. You were saying?"

I opened and closed my mouth again. "A body?" Was I eternally doomed to be interrupted whenever I tried to tell him the truth?

"Yes. I'm sorry to cut our date short, but I need to go to the police station."

The witches immediately surrounded us. "We'll escort you home, Miss Wilkes."

"That's not necessary—" I got to my feet and was more or less frog-marched from the pub and down the road. The last I saw of Nathan, he was detaching himself from the pack of witches before they hurried me back home.

At least none of them followed me into the house when we finally reached it. I unlocked the front door and paused in the darkened hallway, releasing a heavy sigh. Then I took a step forward—

"MIAOW."

I very nearly jumped out of my skin. Fumbling for the light switch, I found I'd almost trodden on Sky sitting in the dark outside the flat door.

"What is wrong with you?" I whispered to Sky. "If you want to reprimand me for walking outside with a murderer on the loose, scaring me to death isn't going to help anyone."

"Miaow." He pawed at my leg. Beneath his other paw lay a piece of muddied paper.

I knelt down and picked it up. "Another treasure map?" Then I saw the writing on the page.

It was the same as the handwriting on the note I'd received inviting me to go under the waterfall.

"They need a fairy next," I read aloud.

That was it. No other words. No clues.

Sky butted into my leg. I got the message and unlocked the flat door.

"I know you're a fairy cat," I muttered to him. "Is that what this is about?"

"Blair?" Alissa stared at me from the sofa as I walked in. "You're not with Nathan. Did it go wrong?"

"You might say that." I let the door swing closed behind me. "We were surrounded by people for our entire date. It was a disaster. A dozen witches cleared out the pub and escorted me home when Nathan got a message telling him to come and look at another dead elf in the forest."

She winced. "Sorry about that. What's that paper? Did Sky decide to rope you into something again?"

I handed her the page, and she read it with a furrowed brow. "Who's 'they'?"

"The killer," I whispered. "I'm sure it is. The killer... they need me."

She lowered the page. "It doesn't say you."

"They're targeting different paranormals," I said. "That's what this is about. A vampire died, a werewolf died... and an elf, I guess, but the method wasn't the same. I don't understand why they 'need' a fairy. To do what with? What could anyone possibly gain from killing me?"

"This note might mean anything," she said. "It might be a fake. I *hope* it is."

"Why would someone need a fairy specifically?" I asked. "Especially if their last victims were a vampire and a werewolf?"

"I..." Alissa trailed off. "I can think of *one* reason, but it's... it's very dark magic. I saw my grandmother had a book out—a reference book on the subject. Maybe she thinks the same." She pulled out her phone and dialled. "She's left her voicemail turned off."

Think, Blair. They need a fairy... Considering the flowers, walking everywhere with an escort might not save me, and I wasn't about to wait for the killer to show up at the door. "The killer. Nobody actually saw them, right? No witnesses."

"Of course not," said Alissa. "But you said yourself, there might be more than one person working together. The police have only arrested Keith so far..."

"Keith was attacked in the woods," I said. "He doesn't remember the attacker, right? Is there a spell to jog his memory? They're bound to let him out for questioning soon. If he remembers who bit him, it might point to our rogue vampire." Why a rogue vampire might need to kill a fairy was a mystery, too, but it was the only tenuous possible link between the various attacks we had.

"There *is* a memory potion that might work," she said, hesitantly. "But the police wouldn't let me give him a strange potion before the interrogation, assuming there'll actually be one. And neither of us would be able to get into the jail even if we weren't tailed by bodyguards everywhere."

"Miaow," said Sky.

I looked at him, then back at Alissa. "You know he got into the flat when the door and windows were locked?"

Her brow crinkled. "He did?"

"He sneaks out all the time," I said. "I think it's a fairy cat thing, the ability to get into places nobody else can. Can you get into the jail?"

Both of us looked at Sky. He licked a paw, giving away nothing.

"Come on, I know you understand me." I crouched down beside him. "The jail. The vampire in jail… Alissa, do you have a picture of him?"

She held up her phone. The photo of her and Keith had been taken at the coffee shop, by the looks of things.

"Miaow," said Sky.

"This is him," I said, pointing to the picture. "He's in jail." I mimed bars. Alissa burst out laughing. "Great to have your cooperation."

"Never go into theatre, Blair," Alissa said.

I gave her an eye-roll, then turned back to Sky. "Can you get into the jail?" The window had been closed, the house under watch, when he'd sneaked in the last time. Fairy cat or not, he definitely had his own kind of magic.

Sky miaowed again. Then dipped his head in acknowledgement. *Gotcha.*

"Right," I said to him. "Wait there. Alissa's going to whip up a potion to take to him. I hope he knows what he's doing," I added to her quietly.

"Me too," said Alissa. "Do they have their prisoners under close watch?"

"That place was so dark, I couldn't tell." I shuddered at the memory. "There aren't guards outside every cell. I doubt they'd be looking for a cat, especially a magical one who can hide himself."

"If you say so." She moved to the kitchen and began rifling through the cupboards for potion ingredients. "This is a last resort, isn't it?"

"Pretty much." Until then, there was nothing to do but wait.

A cat couldn't get arrested, right? *Don't answer that one, universe.*

14

The cat did not get arrested. He came back the following morning and woke me with a prod of a claw and a 'Miaow'.

"What does that mean?" I asked thickly, rubbing sleep from my eyes. The few minutes of rest I'd managed to snatch had been plagued by dreams of being a pixie caught in a net. Thanks for that one, subconscious. Yawning, I scrambled out of bed and went in search of Alissa.

"I think he got into the jail," she said, peeking her head out of her bedroom. "Mission successful."

Sky miaowed and head-butted my leg. I assumed that meant the potion had been deployed as planned.

So now all we needed to do was get in on the vampire's interview, while avoiding World War Paranormal. With no answers from Madame Grey, we were out of options, short of hoping the potion would trigger the vampire's memories of the attack.

Alissa shook her head at her phone. "She won't

answer. Stony Face outside our house won't tell me if she's at the police station or not, either."

I glanced at the gargoyle standing guard outside our window and picked up my own phone. I'd texted Nathan but received no reply, so he was presumably still tied up with the latest elf murder.

My hand faltered. If I had to tell Madame Grey that I was the target, the truth about what I was would come out no matter what, and he'd rather hear it from me than through someone else.

I chewed on my nails as I one-handedly typed a message, then deleted it. Then I typed another one.

"What're you doing?" Alissa asked.

"Nathan," I said. "The note was no joke. They need a fairy. He's going to find out. I think he'd rather I told him myself. Even if it… if it means he doesn't want to see me again."

There was far more than my love life at risk this time around.

"Isn't he keeping his own secrets?" she asked. "That vampire."

"Don't even." I shook my head. "I have zero clues why Lord Anderson is suddenly innocent, if not an accomplice. Of course, it might be misdirection. The killer might have a vampire accomplice he's sending to bite the victims to confuse us. The poison would have been enough on its own, unless the vampire perpetrator got thirsty in the middle of the mission. But I don't believe Nathan would blindly trust a murderer."

The corners of her mouth turned down. "Misdirection? The vampire who died wasn't bitten. I don't think. And I'm starting to remember Madame Grey's notes on paranormal murders. There was a similar case… a few years ago now. Forbidden magic sometimes requires the blood of a vampire, a witch, and others."

"But what *is* this forbidden magic?"

I jumped when my phone buzzed with a message from Nathan, telling me that Madame Grey was indeed at the jail, and Keith had requested to speak to her about the day he'd been bitten. *He must have remembered.* Which meant the potion had worked. *Thank you, Sky.*

"Has he told you to stop freaking out and it's fine?" said Alissa.

"Nope," I said. "He said the police are letting Madame Grey come and talk to Keith, since he remembers what happened. The potion worked."

"So you didn't tell him?"

I shook my head. "I feel like a coward doing this via text, but he'll probably find out from Madame Grey before the day's end anyway."

"Do it,' she said. "Go on. It'll be easier once it's done."

"Isn't that the point?"

I glanced down at my phone's screen. *Hi, Nathan. I don't know how else to tell you this, but I'm not fully human. I'm half fairy.*

I have no excuse for not telling you, but my cat brought in a note last night telling me the villain needs a fairy for the next part of his plan, and I'm the target.

Sorry, Blair.

Alissa leaned over my shoulder and hit send. I yelped and dropped my phone. Sparks shot from my left hand.

Her eyes widened. "Did your hand just…?"

"Not the first time it's happened." I slowly sank to the floor with my hands over my face. "There it is. I took the coward's way out to avoid a face-to-face confrontation in front of a bunch of witches and gargoyles."

"In fairness, it's probably for the best you didn't tell him at your date last night," she said. "I bet the witches deliberately left gaps in the privacy spell. They're notorious gossips."

"That doesn't make me feel much better, to be honest."

I felt more like hiding under the bed than sitting through Keith's interrogation, but if the potion had caused him to remember anything about the attacker, I had to see this through.

My phone buzzed with a message. From Nathan.

Can you send me a picture of the note?

Huh? I stared at the message. "He just... wants me to send him a photograph of the note. The one telling me the enemy's looking for a fairy."

Alissa reached across the coffee table and passed the paper to me. I snapped a picture of it and sent it to him, my nerves jangling with adrenaline, my heart in my throat. He'd said nothing else, nothing to indicate if he was mad at me or disappointed or concerned or —whatever.

Alissa's phone rang. "Finally." She grabbed it. "Hello? Grandma. Yes, we can come over right away. Obviously, we'll bring the gargoyle. Fine. Bye."

She hung up, her face flushed. "We're going to Keith's interrogation. She got us in."

"How?"

"I didn't ask. I think your cat might have done something disgusting in the jail cells and driven everyone out."

"Really?" I turned to Sky, who'd sprawled out on the

sofa as though there wasn't an imminent death threat against his owner. "So when is it?"

"Two minutes."

"Ah." I scrambled to find my boots and bag, my head spinning. Would Nathan be there? He'd seen the second message but hadn't sent a response, and had given no indication of his thoughts on the first one, either. No good news, but no bad news, either.

We hurried to the police station. Sky stayed behind, but I had no doubt he could appear by my side in a second if he thought I needed it. That cat was consistently baffling, if nothing else, but I owed him a few months of petting for what he'd done for us.

Our gargoyle guard tailed us all the way to the police station. Within, the werewolves had gone, and there was no sign of Madame Grey, either. Just gargoyles.

Alissa pointed at Steve's office, from which hushed voices issued. I trod towards the door, and knocked.

Steve answered, ducking his head under the low doorway with a scowl. "You two. Must you keep meddling?"

"I'm the killer's next target," I answered. "As I assume Madame Grey explained to you." I peered into the room, seeing Keith sat in the chair opposite Steve's desk. "He's here to explain what he remembers of the night he was attacked. I'm almost certain it was the same person who killed the vampire and the werewolf. Right, Keith?"

Alissa and I filed into the room behind Steve, and Keith shifted in his seat under our stares.

"I... I remember some things," he said. "But it's blurry. I was in the woods... walking in the woods. And I heard a noise. A rustling, like a wild animal, or something big in the bushes."

"A… vampire?" I gave Alissa an uncertain look.

His gaze dropped. "It… I think it knocked me over. I remember lying on the forest floor, and… and I think it killed me."

"You're not dead," Alissa said. "You… you turned. Are you absolutely certain it wasn't a vampire?"

"That's just it. I don't remember being bitten. I woke up like this." He touched his fingertips to the bite marks on his neck.

Alissa leaned forwards. "The bite marks," she said. "They look… I don't know. There's something plain odd about all this. Are you absolutely certain it wasn't Lord Anderson?"

"Lord Anderson?" he echoed. "What about him?"

"You've met?" I asked.

"Yeah, he's taught me a bit about the change, since Vincent's been busy for the last couple of weeks."

I frowned at Alissa. "What about the bite marks doesn't look right?"

She shook her head. "It's not that I don't believe the story, but I'm not so certain we're dealing with a vampire here at all. It doesn't sound like a vampire attacked you. But if it was that… if it was the monster in the forest, you'd be dead."

He shook his head. "I only remember that. And it's clear, up until… look, I'm not the murderer." He turned to Steve. "I barely remember the first couple of days in the hospital. I definitely wasn't paying any attention when that guy died. I didn't even know where the blood room was. It was brought to me in the ward. By…"

"Her." Steve's gaze snapped to Alissa. "Right?"

"Not just me," said Alissa, not missing a beat. "I don't deal with a lot of vampires, generally, but—now I think about it, the schedule seemed off. I mean, new vampires usually need more time to adjust than you did. Anyway, all vampires are different. I'm not the expert."

"I didn't call you here to debate about vampire feeding times," said Steve. "I intended to get a confession from the murderer."

"Keith isn't the killer," I said. "The real murderer isn't exclusively targeting the werewolves or vampires. We're waiting to hear from Madame Grey to find out why they might be doing this. A vampire died, a werewolf, and now they're after a fairy. I have proof." I held up the note.

"What's that?" Steve asked.

"A note," I said. "I don't know who it's from. But I'm— half fairy. I'm the target."

He looked at me a long moment. "Flying without wings," he muttered. "I knew there was something off about you."

I took a step backwards in case he went for the hand-cuffs. "It's not illegal for me not to tell you. I didn't even know at first. I thought I was a human, then a fairy, then half witch… anyway, half is enough, because there aren't any other fairies living in town." Except for that pixie, but now Steve was actually listening to me, I didn't want to derail the subject. "And I don't know who left me the note, as I said. But I believe it."

Steve gave a dismissive snort. "The killer didn't give you an in-depth description of how he's planning to kill you? It seems convenient that this note made it past security."

"My cat brought it in," I said. "I didn't fake it. You can look at my handwriting and you'll see it's not the same."

"You know… you're right, Alissa," said Keith, whose face had gone paler than usual. He ran a hand over the bite marks on his neck. "These do look a bit odd. I've tested out these—" he flashed his fangs—"And they don't make the same mark."

"What?" I said. "But you *are* a vampire. Someone turned you."

He swallowed. "Bits of it are coming back to me now. The attacker… it ripped my throat out."

I gaped at him, and so did the others. "What?"

"Vampire blood has healing properties," said Alissa, clapping a hand to her mouth. "I knew there was a discrepancy in the hospital records. When a vampire's blood is used to heal a fatal wound, it causes the same effect as being bitten."

"You're saying someone saved my life and turned me in the process?" said Keith faintly.

Lord Anderson. He'd been in the woods. Had he saved Keith, after the monster had attacked and left him for dead? If so, there might not be a vampire involved in the murders at all. If someone was close to death, a vampire's blood could save them.

I looked at Steve. "He's innocent. The beast in the forest attacked him and left him for dead, and a passing vampire saved his life."

"So who the bloody hell is the killer?" Steve wanted to know.

"Very good question," I said. "Also: where *is* Madame Grey? I thought she was here."

"I think she went to the witches' headquarters to look

up whatever spell she thought the killer might be trying to do." Alissa looked at the vampire. "You won't spread this outside, right? The killer doesn't know we've worked out that Blair is the target yet."

"You're assuming the killer walks free?" said Steve.

"Yes." The door bounced off its frame, and Madame Grey entered. "I do. Alissa, Blair—come with me."

"We'll come back," Alissa said quickly to Keith.

"Like hell," said the gargoyle.

One stern glance from Madame Grey shut him up. Then she beckoned us out of the room.

"Alissa, your hunch was right," she said. "The killer's choices match the actions of someone enacting a blood ritual. There hasn't been a similar case in this town in many years, but vampires have long memories. They say that combining the blood of a shifter, vampire, fairy and wizard at the full moon will grant a person the powers of all four combined."

My mouth dropped open. "So it's a wizard? For definite?"

A wizard related to vampires. He hadn't left the town at all. And his monster—if that's what it was—still waited in the forest.

Madame Grey paused, pressing her phone to her ear, then swore softly. "The werewolves are descending on the vampires' territory."

15

Madame Grey whipped her wand from her pocket, waved it, and vanished in a breath of air.

"That's unfair," I said. "It's not like I can—wait, maybe I *can* do the same."

I'd practised the transportation spell enough times, though not with a wand.

"Blair," Alissa said warningly, but I reached into my pocket and grabbed my own wand, mimicking Madame Grey's movements. The next second, we stood on the road outside the vampires' headquarters, behind a group of angry blond werewolves.

Vincent stood on the doorstep, a bored expression on his face as though he'd been interrupted napping rather than facing down a dozen furious-looking werewolves. You had to admire his nerve. Then again, he'd probably lived long enough that nothing fazed him.

"Cease your shouting," he said to the werewolves. "I was sleeping."

"You refused to respond to our claims," growled Chief Donovan. "That means we can only assume one of your people was involved."

"I told you repeatedly that none of my people were, to my knowledge, involved in the murder of one of yours. I also told you that one of my own people was a victim of this killer. I could not possibly have been clearer about it."

"You're lying."

"No," I tried to interject, but wolf voices were loud even when they weren't growling. "I can sense lies—"

Wolf yells drowned out my words. They didn't seem to be listening to each other, let alone anyone else. Vincent, with his own enhanced senses, would be getting an overload right now, but he wore the same bored expression as though a herd of squabbling ducks had wandered in front of his door.

"There's a ritual," I tried to shout. "A blood ritual—"

"If Madame Grey has proof, it'll be at her headquarters," Alissa yelled in my ear. "We don't want to get stuck in the middle of this."

Madame Grey advanced towards the werewolves, and gave us a look telling us to stand back. Probably wise, considering neither of us had vampire speed or the ability to transform into a huge hairy wolf. Even my unpredictable wand was no match for werewolf teeth. And there was no sign of the wizard, nor Lord Anderson—not to mention Nathan. He hadn't texted me again since his weird question following my confession. That struck me as a bad sign.

"This is a diversion!" I yelled at Madame Grey. "The killer—"

Werewolf yowls swallowed my words, and Alissa grabbed my arm again. "We need to go."

"We left our guards at the prison," I pointed out. "Along with Steve. I doubt he can stop this... wizard ritual, but did Madame Grey tell the other witches?"

"If she did, they'll be at their headquarters," she said.

"They might need warning about this." I jerked my head in the direction of the werewolves. "It's that or go home, and I think the wizard is counting on the witches being distracted."

But he hadn't found a fairy yet. As long as I stayed one step ahead of him... we might be able to stop the killer and turn him over to the police before anyone else got killed.

I waved my wand, and we reappeared outside the witches' headquarters. I pushed open the oak doors and ran inside, in the direction of Madame Grey's office.

"Her office is locked," Alissa said. She touched the door and yelped. "Ow. She put a protective ward on the door, too. Bet that's where she left the proof of the ritual she thinks the wizard is doing."

"I guess she took precautions. Wouldn't want anyone else getting ideas."

I put my own hand on the door and winced when a static shock leapt up my arm. Ow. I reached for my wand, wondering if some of the spells Madame Grey had tried on the wards outside the wizard's house would work here, too. I'd spent long enough watching her cast every ward-undoing spell in the book.

"What are you doing?" asked Alissa, as I raised my wand.

"Improvising." I hoped I remembered right, but I'd stood next to Madame Grey for an uncomfortable hour surrounded by vampires, and the spell patterns were kind of burned into my head by this point.

I waved my wand carefully. The door glimmered, and the ward symbols faded.

"No way," said Alissa, putting her hand on the doorknob. "You did it. How?"

"I was copying the spell she used to try taking out the wards on the wizard's house. I don't know what spell it actually was."

"Oh, Blair." She turned the doorknob and opened the door. "Never mind remedial classes. Rita needs to put you into the advanced witchery class, asap."

"That can wait." I stepped into her office. Her desk was noticeably empty. "Did she take the notes with her?"

The lights went out, plunging the whole room into blackness.

My heart kick-started. "Alissa."

"Hmm?"

"Er, you didn't happen to see anyone else on the way in, did you?"

"No."

"This place is warded." I spoke more to reassure myself than anything, but suddenly, even the witches' headquarters seemed oddly quiet. Sure, Madame Grey was absent at the moment, but there was someone far more dangerous than a pack of angry wolves loose in town.

I lunged for the office door, breathing out a sigh of relief when it opened. "We shouldn't be here."

Alissa exited the room behind me. "Blair, do you think the killer came in? Why would he?"

"To steal Madame Grey's notes, or to prove he could? Who knows." I crossed the hall to the oak doors, which rattled in their frame when I pushed against them. "Locked."

Alissa pulled her wand out. "Who's in here?" she said loudly.

Silence answered.

My heart beat rapidly in my ears. "Is there a back exit?"

"This place can't be locked. Madame Grey owns the whole building." She raised her wand and zapped the door with a spell. It didn't budge.

"We're dealing with a powerful wizard here," I whispered. "I bet he stole Madame Grey's research—but he didn't need it. He already has what he needs."

Except for me. I'd undone those wards by sheer luck, and only because the wizard had imitated the same wards that'd been used on his house. Maybe he'd even put them there himself to stop anyone else from getting inside. But he hadn't booby-trapped the place. That was down to the pixie. To stop him from finding anything? Was there something hidden in the mansion after all?

The shadow of a person appeared in the corner of my eye. *Oh no. he's already here.*

There was a flash of glittering light and the pixie appeared in front of us, waving frantically.

"The pixie!" I said. "We need to follow him."

"What? I don't see anything."

"He's on our side." Spinning around, I waved my wand, and a jet of disco-light-coloured paint splattered the entire hall. I grabbed Alissa's arm and dragged her after me into the nearest classroom.

"What's this for?" she gasped as I slammed the door behind us.

"The window." I flung a spell at the window, which splattered it with paint instead of breaking the glass.

Alissa waved her wand, and the window snapped open. I made a mental note to learn that spell, and followed her, the pixie whizzing above our heads making urgent noises. The window required some intense acrobatic work to climb out of and I insisted on Alissa going first, despite her protests.

As Alissa climbed onto the windowsill outside, the door slammed open behind me.

With a shriek, the pixie raised its hands. Glitter poured down, and the wizard yelled in anger as I grabbed the window and hauled myself out. The pixie zipped out behind me, and Alissa pointed her wand at the window, sealing it shut.

"He must have planned for the possibility of getting locked in," I said, shaking paint and glitter off my shoes and wishing I'd used a spell that wouldn't leave such a conspicuous trail.

Alissa waved her wand, making the glitter and paint vanish. "You're right. He's too intelligent to fall for an obvious trick. He must know she'll be back even if the vampires and werewolves go into outright conflict. It was a risk him going there at all, but he must have done something to lure the witches elsewhere. Unless they're all going to prepare for the werewolves' conflict with the vampires."

"He has the research." I began to walk away, determined not to let the pixie out of my sight. "We need to warn Madame Grey. Wolves or none. C'mon."

She followed me, swearing under her breath. "That wasn't a complicated sealing spell. He'll be after us in a second."

"I don't think he's a very powerful wizard, you know," I said. "Otherwise he'd have done worse."

Not that it was much of a consolation. Not only had I been utterly wrong about the killer, I'd left the murderer behind in a place he'd managed to break the wards on once before—somewhere that was supposed to be safe.

The pixie flew ahead of us. "I think he was trying to stop the wizard, too," I said. "Not sure why. But he booby-trapped Lord Goddard's house, probably to stall him."

"What, you think there's something in that house he needs?"

"Maybe."

Glitter flashed in front of us, and the pixie stopped as Sky the cat appeared out of the air. He landed on his feet, casual as anything.

"Wow." I gaped at him. "All right, get Vincent, tell him we're in trouble. If you can't telepathically tell him that, anyway. We'll be right behind you."

There was a faint growling noise. My skin prickled.

"Those wolves are still kicking up a fuss," Alissa remarked.

"That… doesn't sound like a werewolf." My heart beat faster, and I pulled out my wand.

There was a tremendous roar, and an explosion of fur collided with me from the side. Alissa screamed, and I waved my wand wildly. *Levitate.*

At top speed, I flew out from underneath the creature, which face-planted spectacularly in a heap of fur.

Whatever it was, it defied description. Long thick hair

covered a body as big as a werewolf's, and sharp teeth curved from its jaws. A monster. *The* monster. How had it evaded attention for so long?

Alissa raised her wand and cast a spell. The creature shook its head, as though dazed, but didn't stop. The pixie flew overhead, and the creature rose onto its hind legs, batting at the unexpected distraction. I grabbed the wand I'd dropped and cast another levitation spell.

The monster flew into the air. So did Alissa, with a startled shriek, and so did I…

"Nicely done," said a voice, and everything went black.

———

I woke up in a dark room, with a sharp gasp. My thoughts were muddled, my head pounding. *Where am I?*

Piece by piece, it came back. The monstrous creature had been under Peter's control, so if I had to guess, he'd brought us into Lord Goddard's mansion. It was too dark to tell which room, but at least I wasn't a snack for a giant hairy monster. I also wasn't dead.

So he hadn't killed me after all?

I raised my hands in front of my face. Despite the darkness, my hands shimmered oddly. Glitter, faintly green, lit up my skin.

Oh no.

I tried to stand up and tripped. My ankles were bound together, preventing me from using my wings. My *wings.* My glamour must have come off, maybe in self-defence. It'd probably freaked him out. But I'd still been captured and tossed in here, alone.

Where was Alissa?

I crawled towards what I thought might be a door, based on the shadowy outline, and shoved it with my elbows. The glitter on my hands must be good for something, right? But my wand was missing. He must have taken it.

I used magic without a wand before.

I waved my left hand, but nothing happened. Then I kicked the door and received nothing but a bruised foot for my trouble. He'd even removed my boots. From the thin stream of light trickling in from outside, my feet looked smaller than before, my legs, longer. And green. I remembered my nightmares, mirrors with cracked glass and green pointed ears—

Not now, Blair.

"Sky," I whispered. I'd called him before, just by saying his name. But maybe even he couldn't bypass the wards on this place. Assuming he hadn't run off out of self-preservation. The wizard needed a fairy to complete his plan, after all.

"Sky!" I shouted.

There was a flash of glittering light, and the pixie appeared above me.

"You can pass through walls, too?"

The pixie fluttered its wings. It was kind of cute, actually, once you got past the fact that it hadn't been much help against the monster. And that it'd nearly got my hand stuck in a mousetrap the last time I'd been in here.

"Was it you? Did you stop him?" I asked in a whisper.

The pixie vanished as the door opened. I stepped backwards, nearly tripping over my bound feet, and the wizard glowered at me. Neon paint and glitter still covered him, with the overall effect of a walking Christmas tree. I very nearly laughed despite the circumstances. It was plain to see the pixie prankster had been thwarting his plots from the start.

"What's so funny?" he asked.

"I shouldn't have taken so long to guess it was you," I said. "Your 'the evil vampires are out to get me' act never made any real sense."

"Really? And I suppose your attempts to get yourself under protection conveniently disappeared as soon as you wanted to nose around here."

I rubbed my forehead. "I have no idea what you're talking about. You tried to kill me."

"I have no intention of killing you, Blair," he said. "I took the lives of the others I needed because they had no value for me. But you're different. Do you have any idea how rare it is to have a true fairy specimen?"

My stomach turned over. "That's what I am?" I said. "A specimen? You need my blood so you can steal my powers, right?"

"Beforehand, I'd like to understand what your magical talent is really capable of," he said. "It would be much easier if you told me yourself."

Bad luck, because even I don't know.

I spotted my wand sticking out of his pocket. If not for the rope tying my feet together, I might be able to fly fast enough to snatch it up.

I kept my eyes on his face. "You think if you ask nicely, I'll cooperate, even after you kidnapped me?"

"Yes," he said. "I do. Blair, I'm told you're quite agreeable under pressure, as I'm sure your friend will attest."

My throat went dry. "Alissa. What did you do to her?"

"No more than I needed to subdue her."

"You know you're a dead man if Madame Grey gets anywhere near this place, right?" I lowered my hand to my side, readying myself to move fast.

"She'll never be able to catch me. And my pet will take care of the others."

He called that monster a *pet*. "The bite marks," I said. "You wanted everyone to think a vampire killed that werewolf, so you made those marks yourself, didn't you? And with the first victim, you didn't need to leave any clues to make some of them blame the werewolves."

"No," he said. "Poison is a simple method. Impersonal."

And subtle enough to get around my lie-sensing ability, apparently. Not good.

"And you set the vampires and werewolves against one another so nobody would guess you killed your own distant relation," I said. "Why not just ask him, if there was something in this house you needed?"

"I had to make sure he wasn't around to thwart me," he said. "I knew he had the secrets of the blood ritual locked up in here somewhere. I confess I didn't foresee how difficult it would be to obtain that information... even the witches couldn't find it all, in the end."

"So you didn't steal it from Madame Grey's office at all," I said. "You just wanted us to think you did, so you could lay a trap for us."

"In the end, you walked into the bait yourself, Blair," he said. "I'm aware that your allies are likely trying to break down the boundaries to the house right now, but they'll never succeed. I have a transportation spell set up and ready... for both of us. All I need is your blood."

He moved towards me, and I lunged with my bound feet, knocking into him. He grabbed the wall for balance, and I beat my wings, flying at him as fast as I could. As I collided with him, I grabbed the wand from his pocket. Sparks shot from the end and he jumped, swearing at the top of his lungs. The wand had set his jacket on fire.

"Thanks," I said, wand in hand. "Fair warning: I have no idea what I'm doing with this."

Glitter and flames exploded from the wand's end, and he backed away. "Then I'll have to bring in my pet."

He turned and ran, leaving a trail of glitter behind him. The coward was actually running away.

"Alissa!" I shouted, no longer caring if he heard me. "Alissa, where are you?"

Screams came from my left, and I followed the sound down the hallway to another door. One blast from my wand took it off its hinges. Inside the room, Alissa struggled upright, her feet bound in the same way mine had been.

"Does he have your wand?" I asked.

She shook her head. "No, I dropped it outside when he brought us in here."

"He's fetching his pet monster. We need to get out." I crouched to help her undo the bonds on her ankles, and helped her to her feet.

"Did he take your boots, too?" she asked.

"Unfortunately, but I can fly."

Her gaze went to my shoulders. "Yep. I think I might be dreaming."

"Or in one of my nightmares."

The pixie appeared in a shower of glittering dust,

beckoning us to follow. "Definitely a nightmare," murmured Alissa. "I guess he took the glamour off?"

"He's not the only one."

The carpet was coarse against my feet and I'd be treading glitter everywhere for days, but I kept running. We ran into the living room, where my levitating boots lay discarded. I grabbed them, tossing them to Alissa.

"Alissa, put these on," I told her. "I can already fly."

The ground trembled as a roar came from behind us. Alissa's hands fumbled the boots. "Is that thing *inside* the house?"

"I'm guessing yes. Ready to fly?"

"I have no idea how to use these boots!" she yelped.

"The start button's on the heel." At another roar, I flew to the window and waved my wand, causing it to snap open. Alissa yelped as I grabbed her arm, pulling both of us out of the window and onto the lawn.

Glass shattered over us from behind, and Alissa screamed.

"Just fly—the wards should let us out—"

There was a flash of glitter, and Sky appeared in the middle of the lawn. He strode towards us, not at all like we'd just escaped a mad wizard and his pet monster.

"MIAOW."

In place of Sky appeared a giant furry creature—a huge catlike monstrosity with one glowing blue eye, one grey one.

My *cat* was a monster.

Sky roared and jumped past us, right at the pursuing monster. Alissa and I ran—or flew—towards the fence, and freedom. The wizard hadn't lied—there were a number of people gathered outside the wards. They'd probably heard the racket all the way from the vampires' place, and formed a temporary truce to see what in the world was going on here.

The vampires, werewolves and witches all collectively stared at me. Oh, no. Everyone could see what I was. There was no hiding it now.

16

I hovered, wings beating, wishing I could evaporate on the spot, and wishing harder that I had the faintest clue how to turn my glamour back on. I didn't know how it'd come off in the first place. But Nathan—I didn't dare meet his eyes, not wanting to face the distrust and revulsion I knew I'd see staring back. He stood slightly apart from the crowd, but no glamour would hide me from him.

I guess I was still a coward after all.

Alissa moved to my side, still hovering above the ground. That helped. A little.

"Can anyone bring those wards down?" I said.

There came a loud shout from behind. The wizard stormed towards us, still shedding glitter everywhere. "GET BACK HERE!"

"Not happening," I said.

Leaving the limp form of the monster behind, Sky lunged at the wizard, tackling him off his feet. The wizard screamed, high and shrill, but Sky held him pinned down.

"That ought to hold him until the police get here," said Vincent, leaning casually on the fence as though highly entertained. "You're different," he remarked, eying my wings.

"No, I'm the same person I've been all along."

"Killers!" yelled one of the werewolves. They stood in their own group, all wearing disgruntled expressions as though annoyed the vampires had abandoned their imminent battle to come to watch the show instead. I nearly laughed at the sight of Callie's cousin, who seemed more put out that the vampires had run off in their middle of his ranting than he and the others had been about the potential war.

Before anyone could start a fight, the pixie flew past, drawing everyone's eyes. So it'd turned its glamour off, too.

"Hey," I said, beckoning it over. "Can you tell me how to turn my glamour back on? It'd help if people stopped staring at my wings so I can explain how we caught the wizard."

The pixie snapped its fingers, and glitter flew from its hands, straight at me. *Hang on—*

I fell out of the air as my wings disappeared. Luckily, Alissa caught my arm before I fell, using the levitating boots to bring us both down to ground level.

"MIAOW," said Sky, who remained sitting on top of the struggling wizard. Everyone looked at him, instead of my sudden transformation from fairy to human.

A blast from Madame Grey's wand drew the crowd to silence. "We have our killer," she said, indicating the wizard. He flailed feebly, pinned under Sky's giant paw. I hardly believed I'd been living in the same flat as that monster for weeks without knowing what he really looked like. Which part of him was glamoured? Or was he a shapeshifter, like the werewolves?

"He *was* hiding with the vampires," Chief Donovan said accusingly. "They were complicit."

"None of us had any association with that individual," said Vincent. "He was quite rude to us, actually, when we requested entry to his house."

"He inherited that house from one of you!" insisted the werewolf chief.

"By murdering the owner," Vincent said, with a flash of fangs. "I'd suggest keeping your mouth shut until Blair has told us the story."

Once again, everyone turned to look at me. "You saw," I said, with a glance at the flailing wizard. "Peter is the killer. He needed to kill different paranormals... ask Madame Grey if you want to know why. He threw off the trace by pretending to leave town, and trying to turn everyone against one another. He also tried to attack the witches' headquarters, if you need any more proof. And I guess he's been keeping his pet monster in the forest for weeks. Probably to draw the police away." *Note to self: tell Madame Grey that the witches' headquarters is covered in glitter and paint before anyone goes back in there.*

"Speaking of monsters," said Callie's cousin, jerking his head in the direction of Sky the Monster Cat. "Just what is that?"

"My pet cat," I said.

"What I don't get," said Alissa, "is that Peter seemed pretty convinced he didn't send the death threat to our house."

"Oh, he said something like that to me," I said. "I didn't

think at the time, but… I don't know. Maybe he didn't." I looked at the crowd, and spotted Bryan hidden near the back. As he didn't meet my eyes, Alissa stiffened next to me.

"Bryan?" said Alissa. "Did you?"

Bryan looked at his feet. "I didn't want to kill you," he said quietly. "I wanted you under close watch so you didn't run into the killer. I swear. It was supposed to knock you out so you stayed at home."

"And in the hospital?" I asked.

"Not then. I didn't know."

"They weren't the same flowers," said Alissa. "I'd thank you, but you nearly got my friend killed. They're poisonous to fairies."

"I didn't know she was—did anyone know?" He looked around as though expecting someone to deny that I'd transformed in front of them, but everyone seemed more interested in Sky the Monster Cat, and the still-struggling wizard.

"So Bryan left the flowers," I said. "Anyone else unaccounted for?"

"Yes," snapped Chief Donovan. "If the killer was a wizard, why were there bite marks on the dead werewolf's body?"

"Because the killer wanted to hide his traces," I said. "And stoke tensions between you and the vampires. Vampire bites probably aren't that hard to fake, not if he knew the werewolves would conclude that the bite marks belonged to a vampire without looking too closely."

"Wasn't there a rogue vampire in the woods?" asked Chief Donovan, refusing to be deterred.

"Yes," said Lord Anderson. "I bit someone in the forest."

Shouts and exclamations ensued from the werewolves.

"You attacked one of us!" yelled Callie's cousin.

"Monster!"

"Murderer!"

"A wizard," he said, his voice rising. "He was attacked by the creature that wizard kept in the woods, I'd guess. I found him dying and I chose to save his life. In the process, I turned him. I take full responsibility for what I did. I didn't take a life in the forest: I saved one."

The exclamations continued, only to cease at a second explosion of noise from Madame Grey's wand.

"You turned a human against his will," she said.

"Yes," Lord Anderson said. "I confess. I did. I'll take punishment as the vampire council sees fit."

Nathan said, "I can back him up. He confessed what he did, when I confronted him over the murders."

So that was his big secret. And he still hadn't looked at me.

Vincent stepped in. "I will handle the matter myself. As for the killer, he won't be getting out of there." He passed through the gates into the grounds, leaving a faint shimmering behind.

I frowned at him. "What did you do?"

He smiled, showing pointed teeth. "I changed the settings on those wards using my own blood. You can all get out, but the wizard can't."

"He has a transportation spell."

"Not for long." He tilted his head, and I turned around. Sky the Monster Cat had disappeared, while several gargoyles flew over the fence to surround the dazed-looking wizard.

Alissa nudged me. Sky sat at my feet, back to normal size.

"Miaow?" I said.

"Miaow," Sky agreed.

What a spectacle we'd made. The vampires hung around watching the wizard's arrest, while the were-wolves had already begun to slope away, some of them still looking disgruntled. The gargoyles paid no attention when I walked out of the grounds, Sky purring at me the whole way. "Thanks," I whispered, stroking him behind the ears. "I'm glad the war's off."

"Tell me about it," said Alissa. "Er—do you want these boots back? I can conjure my shoes back from the mansion."

I looked down at my shoe-less feet. "Oh, yeah. Sure."

While Alissa pulled off the boots, I turned back to watch the gargoyles haul the wizard to his feet. I hoped that monster of his was dead, even if it freaked me out that Sky could transform into an equally scary beast.

I don't think I'm going to need a security guard again.

Once I'd tugged my boots back on, Alissa gave me another urgent nudge. I turned, seeing Nathan walking away, separate from the crowd.

Guess it was up to me, then.

I headed over to him. "Nathan," I said. "I'm sorry. I wanted to tell you. Before. I..."

He finally looked at me. "You know... I think I knew. Deep down."

That this was never going to work? "I didn't know at first,"

I said honestly. "Blythe did—god knows how—but she led me to believe I was all fairy, and not a witch at all. I thought I'd get kicked out of the town for deceiving the witches. When I found out I was a witch after all, I hoped I'd be able to put it behind me. It's not like I've actually met my fairy relatives."

"No," he said. "But it strikes me that an awful lot of other people seem to know. Veronica... Madame Grey... even Lord Anderson."

"He... told you?" So he'd known the whole time.

He nodded. "Veronica clued me in the moment she hired me, but I thought I'd give you the space to work through it alone."

My heart seized on the word *alone*. I'd told everyone *except* him. "Sorry," I said, again. "I thought you'd been through enough of my drama without me adding *that* on top of it. Mr Falconer, the murder attempts, having to play security guard outside my house..."

"I didn't mind doing any of that, Blair," he said. "It's your business. I shouldn't have implied you needed to tell me all your secrets.

Ouch. "I didn't intend the whole town to know either," I said. "Blythe read it from my mind without my permission. Same with the vampires. And the witches all found out by accident when Rita used a spell to divine my magic type. The rest was on me. And I really should have... I should have told you." I drew in a breath. "Does this mean you don't want to see me again?"

"No," he said. "But I don't think it's a good idea at the moment."

My heart free-fell. "Okay. I understand."

"Not because of what you are," he said. "But because I haven't been entirely honest with you either, Blair."

"I—why?" My palms went sweaty.

"That note you received," he said. "I wondered… when I saw the handwriting. I was sure I recognised it."

My insides pitched downwards. "You recognised it? How?"

"I've seen it before," he said. "When I used to work for the hunters."

What? "You… why?"

"There's another paranormal prison, further north," he said. "I used to work there as security, for a time. I remember your father was brought in, before he was transferred somewhere else. He… I'm sorry, Blair, but I don't know why he was arrested, or where they took him afterwards. But the writing is his. I remember he left a note with the staff."

"My father. You… had him arrested?" I was having a nightmare. This was one of my weird fairy dreams. It couldn't be real.

"I'm sorry, Blair," he said. "I didn't know he had a daughter. I don't normally talk to the prisoners, but that particular incident stuck in my memory."

I opened and closed my mouth. Nope, no words.

"Anyway, I thought you deserved to know."

I stood frozen, barely aware of Alissa moving to my side. At that, he gave me a brief look I couldn't read, then walked away.

"Blair?" said Alissa. "What did he—?"

I shook my head. I couldn't say it.

The paranormal hunters might have arrested my only living family.

———

"You look terrible," said Alissa, accosting me in the kitchen the next morning.

If I looked half as bad as I felt, I wasn't fit for human company. I couldn't remember the last time I felt this wretched, including being number one on a killer's hit list. At least then I'd had hope that things would work out with Nathan.

"Ugh." I sighed. "I know, I know, I brought this on myself. Still hurts."

"You couldn't have guessed he…"

I'd told her the truth when we'd made it back home yesterday, after shaking off Madame Grey and the other people curious to speak to the town's resident fairy. I didn't need a lie-sensing power to tell Nathan felt bad for having to break the news, and he'd only been doing his job. The paranormal hunters wouldn't have arrested someone without reason, right?

"Don't worry about it," I said. "Maybe if I keep saying it aloud, I'll eventually get halfway over him. I just wish I knew where they… they took my father. Or what was in the note he left."

So who had been leaving the notes inviting me to speak to them? Someone who knew my family? Or that pixie? I hadn't seen it since yesterday, but there'd been a lot of ugly crying last night, and it'd probably wanted to leave me in peace.

No. I didn't blame Nathan. I blamed *me*, for not telling him the truth from the outset, and the fact that he'd known all along made things even worse. He'd seen me without glamour. He must think I was a freak, at the very least.

"What about… you and Keith?" I asked Alissa.

"We're taking a break," she said. "Considering everything that's happened, he has a lot to adjust to. As for me, I think I'll swear off dating for a while."

"Me too. At least the whole town knows what I am now, so there'll be no more unwelcome surprises."

"It's not the end," Alissa said firmly. "He just needs time to process. So do you. Put it on hold until both of you are in the right state of mind."

"Normally I'd say you're right, but he did kind of lock up my family. We have to address that at some point, otherwise I'll never be able to stop wondering. I don't know. I never met my father. But part of me really wants to think he's innocent. Nathan told the truth when he said he didn't know where he'd been taken, but still, he has contact with the other hunters. He can probably find out. Is it bad that I want to contact him again, just for that?"

"I don't blame you," she said. "We might be able to get the full story…"

"What, by stalking Nathan? That won't help. Besides, I don't know where the actual collective of paranormal hunters operates from, only that they live north of the lake."

Her expression turned thoughtful. "I could ask my grandmother. There's little she doesn't know about when it comes to the citizens of the town. With a background like his, I'm sure she asked him a lot of questions. To make sure he wouldn't act against innocent citizens. The others… the hunters in general don't mix with paranormals on a casual basis like he does."

"Yeah, I'm starting to see why," I said.

"He never actually said he'd hold it against you," she said.

"He may as well have." I shook my head. "Even if he doesn't, we still deceived one another pretty thoroughly. That's not a good basis for a relationship."

"You're not wrong, but maybe you should talk to him again, when you're not in such a precarious position. I think he was pretty shocked when you took the glamour off."

"So am I," I said. "My father. He's—alive. Maybe my mother is, too. And I doubt the other hunters will easily tell me where he's locked up."

"No, I suppose not. But we can find out."

I blinked at her. "You're set on this, aren't you? How would we even begin to get into a paranormal prison, even if we managed to find it?"

"You do own a fairy cat who can walk through walls, don't you?"

"Yeah…" I looked around for Sky. "Speaking of whom, I'm sure he knows when I need him." He'd only left my side after I'd cried myself to sleep, and had seemed weirdly tolerant of my sobbing into his fur.

"Miaow," came the faint noise from the bedroom.

I frowned and walked to the door, then froze. In the crack between door and wall, I glimpsed Sky on the bed, pinning the pixie beneath one paw.

"Don't!" I flung the door wide and made a lunge for the bed. Sky let go of the pixie, who spun in circles, shedding glitter everywhere. Before I could catch him, he made a beeline for the window and fluttered out of sight. "Oh, no."

"Blair!" Alissa pointed to the bed, where a crumpled note lay.

I picked it up, my heart beating against my ribcage.

I apologise for failing to meet you the other day. As a fairy, I have permission to leave the LFPF on two days per year—the summer and winter solstices—as they are important events for us. While I would have been accompanied by prison guards, I very much wanted to see you, but I understand that the town was in considerable danger. I'm very glad to hear that the danger has passed and that you are safe.

If you want to contact me, send word with the pixie.

The note wasn't signed.

My mouth hung open for a moment. "I… I don't know how to make sense of this, but… I think it might be from my father." Which meant he'd been the one to leave the other notes.

Alissa took the paper from my hand, exclaiming, "The LPFP. Lancashire Prison for Paranormals. You're right. He mustn't have signed the note in case it fell into the wrong hands."

I nodded mutely.

Alissa went on, "So they let him out at the solstice… I think the solstices are important to fairies, for some reason. That's what my grandmother said."

"She didn't tell *me* that. Oh, never mind. My father's locked up, and now it turns out he *did* want to see me, it's nearly six whole months until the next solstice."

"I think that cat of yours can deal with the situation," she said. "He got that note to you somehow, right?"

"Or the pixie."

I looked at the window, then at Sky. "I hope you didn't scare him off for good."

"Miaow." Sky jumped off the bed and rubbed himself against my legs. He couldn't have said *you're my human* more obviously if he'd spoken aloud.

Despite myself, I found myself smiling. "You know, I think we might be okay."

ABOUT THE AUTHOR

Elle Adams lives in the middle of England, where she spends most of her time reading an ever-growing mountain of books, planning her next adventure, or writing. Elle's books are humorous mysteries with a paranormal twist, packed with magical mayhem.

She also writes urban and contemporary fantasy novels as Emma L. Adams.

Find Elle on Facebook at https://www.facebook.com/pg/ElleAdamsAuthor/

www.ingramcontent.com/pod-product-compliance
Lightning Source LLC
Chambersburg PA
CBHW020810190726
48285CB00006B/2233